RAMBLIN' RANTS AND DOGGIE TALES

by

J.D. ROGERS

ODYSSEY PRESS
Fallbrook, California

Odyssey Press
1842 Santa Margarita Drive
Fallbrook, CA 92028
shorecam@aol.com

ISBN #978-0-938297-21-5

Cover photo by David Gibb

To my parents

Jim and Shirley Rogers,

who rescued me from under a turnip leaf.

I love you.

Acknowledgements

Bravo and thanks to the following folks who were co-conspirators in the antics and many depraved adventures of my life. And a radiant applause to those who helped turn my rants and ravings into this cohesive book.

The late Fred Radcliffe—the man who altered my life by taking me on my first trip to Moab, Utah; who showed me how to cook baked beans on the engine of a moving Volkswagen, though sometimes the can does blow up.

The late, great Larry Cosby—a man of many talents, whose side I sat by for more than a decade as he did the Applegater layout. When I asked him to do something special, he would tell me he was "just a technician, not a magician." The material for this book would never have been found if Larry did not have a map in his own mind of where everything was hiding.

Indiana Home boys: Boyd Uselton—what other musician would own a 1962 Studebaker Lark with watermelon green fenders and all the other parts painted hot pink and covered in psychedelic stick-on flowers? I know, Mardy Wilson would. It is scary to think I know two people who owned this car. Fate had thrown us together into several bands where we knew we were destined to be rock stars.

Some of the Utah outlaws: Rick Costanza—for sharing his hunting grounds in Arches Monument (now a national park) and the 13th hole of the local golf course. His name can now be found in Webster's Dictionary as part of the definition of "deranged."

The late Ken Hoffman—who showed me that working at the potash mines evaporation ponds could be fun as long as you worked at the glue-dispensing barrel; for splitting my five-dollar-a-week trailer rental, which included utilities, and sleeping on the couch, thus leaving me the bed; and for the eviction from said trailer due to his never-ending stream of girls and beer passing through our place.

Robert Ossana—for showing me that mountain bikes were for wimps and all you needed was a good three-speed. I had been warned to steer clear of him when I moved to Moab, but I was drawn to him like a moth to a light. The song "Bad Reputation" describes him best.

Chris Allen—for encouraging me in my illegal gun-running career after his inspection of my merchandise, and for his participation in the scattering of our brain cells to the most remote canyons in the southwest.

Michael Pearce—for the brain damage I incurred from riding in the back seat of his Datsun 510 that had no exhaust system for hundreds and hundreds of miles, and for introducing me to good old Jim Beam.

Al McLeod—for sharing the adventure of running the rapids on the Colorado River under a full moon, that is, until a cloud cover comes in and you have dead batteries in your flashlight; and what a tag team we were at the ladies' hat parties.

My publishers Patty Campbell and David Shore—for believing that anyone would want to read my rants and ramblings, and for their patiently staying with me through all of my indecisive moments.

Barbara Holiday—for her creative and expert editing skills, for being the greatest layout girl, and especially for her always-ready munchies and fabulous martinis as dry as her sense of humor.

My dogs Tuesday, Utah, Boogie, Bentley and DooDoo—whose unconditional love, companionship, and ongoing antics have given me lifelong writing material.

Weston Taussig, who is like a son to me, and not only thinks I am tall, but is the best audience, a depraved storyteller could ever want; for staying up with me all night, and writing the next best horror movie about ticks; and lastly for loaning me his skirt because, well, I really needed it.

And finally to my beloved bride Sioux—who not only believes in me as a mad rock 'n roller and a mountain man, but she also thinks I am tall, she has never laughed at my inability to spell, and she continues to love me in spite of all my disgusting habits.

TABLE OF CONTENTS

INTRODUCTION – WHO IS THIS J.D. ROGERS?

J.D. Rogers was born a Hoosier in Indianapolis, Indiana in 1951. He attended Avon High School, where he majored in study hall, home room, and the principal's office. Dress codes were not to J.D.'s liking. Why did an unaccredited high school like Avon care if he wore paisley-colored capes with knee-high suede boots? Besides, with his band, he was destined to be a rock star—or so he thought.

After barely graduating from the high school where the principal had once suggested, "It would be best for all concerned, J.D., if you just quit school," he went to work for a few months in a factory that manufactured heating and cooling systems. It was during this brief internment that it became obvious to J.D. that he had two choices: suicide or a move to Moab, Utah. Moab was a place he'd been in love with since his first visit there in the spring of 1964, when he was in the seventh grade. Moab is the land of great arches and broken dreams, deep mysterious canyons, three-legged coyotes (too many trappers), and high-grade uranium ore—a substance that miners carried in their front pockets for self-sterilization and paid for later with testicular cancer.

Moab was home to The 66 Club, The Lrae Club, The Wagon Wheel, Woody's, and the Westerner Grill. It was the place with majestic snow-capped mountains (Mt. Tukuhnikivatz in particular), the Colorado River, Dewey Bridge, Dead Horse Point, and Behind the Rocks. It was the land of outlaws, many of whom would become J.D.'s lifelong friends (most are dead now and others close to it). He continued playing in rock bands, working in uranium mines, and feeding his unquenched addiction to the red rock country, a period he jokingly calls "a life of total debauchery".

After sixteen years he moved to a place he refers to as "the land of curdled milk, rancid honey, and deadly drive-by shootings,"—Los Angeles, California, where he worked hard at pursuing the life of a Rock Star. There he became the only hard rocker in his circle to study organic gardening between gigs.

On the bad advice of a trusted music publisher, J.D. started writing country music. Over the years he recorded three CDs—none even made the discount bins, although they have been sighted at Goodwill Thrift Stores. It appeared that music wasn't in the cards at that time.

But the best thing that came out of his L.A. experience was meeting his "bride," Sioux. After they were married and spent some time in L.A., they bought an eighty-nine-year-old log cabin on forty acres in Applegate, Oregon. The place was a run-down sheep spread that they transformed into magical flower gardens, vegetable beds, and an heirloom apple orchard. It took many gopher traps (the only good gopher is on a coat collar) to make this place in paradise happen. Nowadays they slave happily at the ranch with their current beloved dogs--two rescued Border Collies, Tuesday and Utah—backed up by Chloe the calico cat and dozens of chickens.

Promo shot of "3 fifty 7" band members: Randy Sackerson, Mark Wilkerson, Dave "Twisted" Jaynes, Johnny Capatto and JD Rogers   1979

And now J.D. introduces The Applegator:

This book is the result of fourteen years as editor of *The Applegator*, a small community newspaper in Southwestern Oregon. The tales are true as far as I can remember. They cover a lifetime. Those who are mentioned by name were there and are just as guilty as I am. I find everyday events the best fodder for my ramblings in my bimonthly columns.

The Applegator is a nonprofit publication that was published by the Applegate Partnership, from August 1994 to April 2008. The Partnership was formed in 1993 in response to the timber wars here in the Pacific Northwest. It was a time of spotted owls vs. loggers. From the beginning the Partnership was made up of loggers, environmentalists, ranchers, Forest Service and Bureau of Land Management representatives, academics, and just plain old interested folks who knew we could have owls and still remove some timber from the woods. *The Applegator* was the avenue to get information on riparian restoration, thinning from below, reforestation, fire management, fuel reduction, and wildlife habitat improvement to the residents in our half-million-acre watershed, which lies in two states (Oregon and California), three counties (Jackson and Josephine in Oregon; Siskiyou in California), with five different resource managers from the U.S. Forest Service and Bureau of Land Management.

The Applegator is now published by Applegate Valley Community Newspaper LLC, a nonprofit organization. The spelling of the name of the paper has been changed to *The Applegater*. To date I've been the only editor *The Applegator/Applegater* has had. I got the job by default (be careful what you volunteer for). Long live rock . . . and enjoy the tales.

JD kicking back in the front porch rocker after a long day working on the Applegator newspaper, 2000.

Star Thistle

When my bride Sioux and I first moved into our place here on Thompson Creek, we named it Rocky Thistle Ranch. There wasn't much we could do about the rocks, but I planned to weed star thistle into extinction. On our place I gathered unsuspecting troops. Whenever we had company, before there would be breakfast, any sightseeing, or opening of the bar, we'd all be in the pasture, crawling around on our hands and knees, weeding these unfriendly trespassers. I did have to do some training though. Some folks would grab star thistle by the top and scream, ******!!!! (They couldn't play guitar very well after that.) I would then show them how to pluck it from the base, root and all, and bag it up if a flower head even thought about showing the color yellow.

After a number of years, and a lot fewer visitors, we had defeated star thistle and his buddies bull thistle and teasel. I still find a couple of pesky trespassers each year, but they meet with a swift end. In fact, I won't even buy star thistle honey, because I'm afraid if we ever eradicate it, some group will start hollering that their industry has gone belly-up, and then the government will demand star thistle be reintroduced. I have nightmares about this.

I've now declared war on the "Velcro" weed (as I call it), known to many as beggar's lice. I know whoever invented Velcro had walked through a patch of this freeloading, hitchhiking nuisance. This stuff is so bad I can't take our two Australian shepherds, Boogie and Bentley, hiking in the woods around our place unless I want to spend hours combing out the sticky little seeds in their matted ears, legs, and undersides. By God, there should be a law against this Velcro weed!

I thought about having leather suits made up for Boogie and Bentley so I could take them hiking, but it would be too much trouble lacing them up in their body suits, legs chaps, and face guards. But on the good side, with them being Australian Shepherds, dogs who have no tails, that would be one less piece of leather to worry about. No, it's just out and out war, now that I'm a seasoned star thistle eradicator.

Cookie Crumbs

It amazes me how fast the holidays passed by. I love the holiday season. It takes so long for the holidays to get here, then with a blink of an eye, they're over. Bummer! I stretch the holiday season out by putting our outdoor Christmas lights up in the house. I never understood stringing lights up outside where you can't see them (unless you have a hot tub outside). Come evening when it's wintery cold, I can sit in front of my wood stove in a room immersed in twinkly lights. ("Twinkly," now there's a word that I have never liked. It has such a wimpy sound to it.) Anyway, it's the middle of January, and I'm still watching my twinkly lights. Heck, we leave our lights up all year long. That way we can enjoy the holiday feeling in July.

The only thing this holiday season lacked for me was that the rock band AC/DC still hasn't come out with a Christmas tape. How I long to hear them sing "Silent Night," "Deck the Halls," or "White Christmas." Every year I wait for them to do a Christmas album, every year—nothing. So I sit back and listen to my old Bing Crosby holiday tapes.

About this time of year all my Christmas cookies are gone. I try to stretch them out, but who's kidding whom here. I open the cookie jar lid one hundred times and ninety nine times, I eat a cookie. So before you can shake a cat's tail (I wonder where that expression came from) there is the hundredth time, and it's over, they're done, they're gone.

My cookies did last longer than the box of bones Sioux bought for Boogie and Bentley. She wrapped the box up real pretty, with a bow and everything. Well, a few days before Christmas, on one of our adventures to town, we left both dogs in the house. That's right, when we returned a few hours later, there was their Christmas present, open and eaten. A few morsels remained among the wet paper and chewed-up bow. However, I was amazed at how carefully they had stepped over all the other presents, even the empty boxes that I wrap up so that it looks good under the tree, to get to theirs at the back. None of the other presents had so much as been moved. Now, that's a feat, seeing that their box of bones was buried under all the other presents. Anyway, both dogs thought they were in trouble for *our* mistake. Do you put chocolate under the nose of a chocoholic?

Boogie and Bentley both began retraining me from that point on. Yes, they talked me into sharing my cookies with them. They would give me those poor pathetic "woe is me" looks as I'd sit dunking my cookies. So I'd get a bite, and each dog would get a bite. That means they got two-

thirds of all my cookies. Oh yes, it's the season to share--
right? Why do I feel that I've been suckered again?

*Bentley—maybe now I'll be able to play the game
"fetch JD's glasses and see what I am looking for,"
1998*

"Fetch It"

I had enjoyed a great pizza for lunch, but by late afternoon, lunch had turned to the miseries. I crawled into bed and managed to drift off to la la land. When I woke up, my glasses were nowhere to be found. Now, I knew I had put them on the night stand by the bed, like I always do, but noooo glasses.

After searching with bleary vision for awhile, I called in the rescue team--our dogs Boogie and Bentley. They have the noses for this kind of work. After all, they always find the rubber carrot.

"Fetch, fetch my glasses, you guys!" But all I got from Boogie and Bentley were stares. They perked up their ears, cocked their heads, and looked at me with that smile that says, "This guy is nuts."

Well, I wasn't going to let this get me down. If the dogs could fetch a rubber carrot, a ball, and a barbecued pig's ear, they could fetch my glasses. I brought out my sunglasses, put them in Boogie's mouth, and told them "Fetch my glasses!" Then I hid them like I do with their ball or carrot and commanded, "Fetch the glasses!" But all they fetched was the carrot. We repeated this scene over and over, and all I got were sunglasses covered with dog drool and teeth marks. I now realized that I might have to put up with bleary vision for a spell.

But aha! Sioux turned up my glasses in no time. It's amazing how good wives are at finding things that their husbands have lost. Sioux has gotten really good at this over the years, thank God. She said my glasses were a few feet from where I knew I had put them.

Boogie and Bentley are going into a "Fetch the Glasses Training Program." It would be just my luck though, that they would fetch me a couple of glasses filled with beer. Heck, that would be great! But just to be on the safe side, I think I'll train them to fetch my car keys and my wife. And maybe brain retrieval would be a good skill too.

Whose Watermelon Is It Anyway?

Life in the Applegate sure is good. I'm kicked back in my rocker on the front porch, drinking in all the beauty around me. Our garden is a rainbow of colors with the hundreds of plants Sioux and I have put in over the years. The columbine and bearded iris (two of my favorites) are exquisite, with colors from white to almost black and all the blues, pinks, purples, oranges, and yellows in between. There are just enough lilacs left to scent the air around me, and with Tallowbox Mountain in the background, today is almost heaven.

Speaking of heaven, I jumped the gun and already bought a watermelon. I wasn't expecting much since they're out of season, so imagine my surprise at the rich, sweet flavor, not to mention all the juice running down my chin. Both our dogs eyed each bite I took as if they'd been fasting for days. I offered Boogie a bite, and it was gone in a snap of the finger (luckily the finger wasn't gone). Bentley wasn't as quick about his nibble, but he knew it was supposed to be good because his mother Boogie said so. From this point on, I got one in three bites for myself. I had a dog's head lying on each knee, saying "Me next!" I was surprised that the hummingbirds that were fighting at the feeder weren't trying to cut me out of another share of watermelon.

Do any of you other folks out there have dogs who like fruit? We know when our grapes are ripe because Boogie and Bentley graze every one that is within reach. It's the same with our raspberries. Luckily, only Boogie goes after the strawberries (sometimes).

So now it's time to take my hollowed-out half watermelon rind to the chickens and abandon the comfort of my rocker to crawl around on my hands and knees and weed this beautiful garden.

Boogie and Bentley catch me trying to eat watermelon behind their backs.

My Left Leg

It was six a.m., and I had the lawn mower oiled, gassed, and ready to go. I could tell it was going to be a hot one that day ('cause the radio told me so). The dogs watched me make a few passes on the front lawn before they retreated to the front porch for the first of many naps they get to take each and every day. It must be a nice life to just sleep, eat, sleep, get petted, eat, and sleep some more, while I work up a sweat.

While I was pushing the mower, it threw up a little rock that stung to high heaven when it hit my bare leg. Now, I never wear shorts when I mow the lawn, but that day I did, and lived to regret it. Good God, it wasn't a rock--I was standing on a yellow jackets' nest and the little boogers were all over my knee! I abandoned the mower and sprinted to the other side of the yard. Luckily, the yellow jackets were moving slowly as the morning was still cool, but my left leg was heating up quickly. I counted one, two, five, nine bites from those godless varmints.

Well, I was really ticked off now, as I watched my left leg turn red and start to swell while I hobbled around the yard. "By God, this is war!" I told the dogs. I retrieved the mower (aren't dogs supposed to do the retrieving?) and headed for the garage to fill a small can with gasoline. Stumbling my way back to the site of the attack, I poured the gasoline down the hole into their nest. I wondered if these actions would put me on the EPA's most wanted list. Who cares, this was war. I lit a match and flipped it into the yellow jackets' hole to send those vermin where they belonged!

I took some antihistamines and had barely finished the front lawn when they kicked in. I hoped none of the neighbors saw me drooling as I crawled off to the house. It was obvious I would be worthless for the rest of the day (but there are those who would say "So what's new?").

Next morning I was ready to go, with my itching basketball-size knee; I *had* to finish the lawn. I was in action by six a.m., mowing down by our barn, when it happened again. I mean who wrote this script? I wanted a new part! Heck, I wanted out of my contract—this had become a horrible B-movie. Yes, yellow jackets were inside my sock, cannibalizing my ankle. I couldn't believe this was happening again. I hopped around hollering, untying my shoe, and trying to take my sock off. The dogs thought this was great fun, some sort of new game, as they ran around me barking, "Let's play!" Some fun--three more bites on the ankle of my still decrepit left leg.

Without hesitation I headed up to the garage, filled my little can with gasoline, grabbed the wasp spray, and nuked the little monsters. I didn't care what rules or laws I'd broken at this point; in fact, I wished I had a little neutron bomb to use on those flying cannibals. I used the wasp spray for picking off all the yellow jackets that flew around their burning bunker. I had to be careful though--that wasp spray was very flammable, as a few yellow jackets found out. Eeeeyaaaa!

Skunked

No, I had not been on a fishing trip to the great state of Alaska. Nor had I been on a hunting trip to the La Sal Mountains in Utah.

I had just returned from a late movie in Medford. As I got out of my truck, I took time to watch the stars dancing in the most magical of night skies. I've never understood why so many people are afraid of the dark. The only light I was seeing came from the stars (city lights spoil a good country night).

Anyway, Boogie and Bentley were whining inside the house, "Come on, Dad, let us out!" When I did, I was met by two pooches whose bodies shook with excitement. I really enjoy this greeting they give me. Think about it—who is always glad to see you, no matter what you've done? Your dog(s), of course! My sweet bride, Sioux (who was out of town) is usually glad to see me, but she doesn't jump up and down and throw herself at my feet (that sounds good). I do believe dog is man's best friend.

I entered the house and turned on a light. Like a flash, Boogie ran back in past me, all wild-eyed and frothing at the mouth. Good God! Was she rabid? What's that smell? *Skunk!* Before I could grab Boogie, she was in the living room rolling on the carpet, her paws pulling at her face, trying to wipe off what had been a direct hit. I grabbed her by the collar and was opening the door to put her out, when Bentley lunged between us, breaking my hold on Boogie, and then both were in the living room trying to transfer their stench onto the carpet. Well, that was just great—two skunked dogs. My eyes were burning from the stench that by now had permeated the house. I finally got both dogs outside and headed back into the house to get our secret weapon for such an occasion, "Super CD" (it removes all odors). Rummaging through drawer after drawer, I finally found it, but the bottle was as dry as the Sahara Desert. Bummer!

I opened all the windows and doors to air the house out, but that was a fruitless effort. What I needed to do was burn the carpet, but I didn't think Sioux would appreciate such an act.

Feeling drained and tired (it was now after midnight), I decided to deal with all of this in the morning. I got two cookies for the dogs, and put Boogie and Bentley in their outdoor kennel for the night. Now, I'd never before made them stay in their prison all night. I told them they'd be better dogs for it, but they didn't buy it.

I crawled into bed, trying to breathe only through my mouth. As I was lying there in the dark, Boogie and Bentley broke into the most lonesome, "end-of-the-world, I-have-just-died" howls that I had ever heard. After a few minutes of this, I started to get up to quiet them down, but suddenly their heartbreaking cries stopped. They're used to sleeping with me when Sioux is gone, so I guess they were telling the world about the cold, gloomy kennel they were stuck in for the night.

As for me, I had dreams all night about working in a sewer plant, cleaning dump tanks with a toothbrush!

Three Dog Night

Our family here at Rocky Thistle Ranch has grown by one. Sioux was just beaming from head to toe when she came home the other night.

"Isn't she cute?" Sioux said to me.

Yea, yea, but where is she going to sleep; we don't need another mouth to feed; my God, all the training I'll have to do. I don't know if we should keep her. By the way, what did you name her?

"Tuesday!"

"Tuesday? I don't like that name at all. Couldn't you call her Stormy, Lucky, or Arco?" I think that would be a good name. After all, it was at an Arco gas station that all this business started. But I am overruled, and Tuesday is to be her name.

Sioux had stopped for gas at an Arco station in Williams, California. There in the middle of a torrential downpour it happened--soaked to the bone and watching each car go by was a six or seven-month-old puppy, a Border Collie, to be exact. Sioux asked the attendants who owned the dog. Nobody knew. She was told that the puppy had been sitting there for four or five hours watching everyone come and go. She gathered up the wet puppy, who had no collar, tattoos, or other means of identification. So Sioux, being Sioux, left her work phone number, the number where she would be staying in San Francisco, and our home phone, and put "Tuesday" in the car with her. Of course, no one called.

Not wanting a negative reaction from me, Sioux started to break the news to me slowly. First, she called home.

"Honey, I've got a surprise for you!"

Well, I love surprises so I was immediately all ears. What could it be? Sioux always gets me the coolest surprises. I asked her what it was, then I said, "Don't tell me," and then "Oh, come on, tell me what it is." Then she let go with the announcement that she had found a puppy.

"She's so cute!"

What was this? An early April Fool's joke? Good try, but I wasn't falling for that. So Sioux called some of our friends to enlist them in the "Let's Keep the Puppy Committee." Over the next week they'd call and say, "Sioux is bringing home a puppy! You'll just love her, J.D."

I thought, "Sure, yea, she's got you guys trying to scam me." Wrong! Sioux got home a few days before Christmas with little Tuesday

Our other dogs finally are getting used to her. Boogie still bars her teeth at the puppy, but Tuesday just licks Boogie's teeth and gums. Bentley tried to hide in the corner for a few days, but they both play together now. As for me, after a few kisses from Tuesday, she has a new home. She knew I'd be easy. As I finish this column, Sioux is down south, the dogs are curled up on the bed, and it's the coldest night of the year—definitely a "Three Dog Night!

Boogie, Tuesday and Bentley in the swing of things, 1997.

Traumatized

It was a great southern Oregon day, just made for splitting firewood. The sun was out; the sky was blue; spring bulbs were starting to show their heads. Yes, it was a magnificent day, except that I had to split firewood (I lied earlier). I hate splitting firewood; it's rugged. For example, the splitting mauls all have handles made for dwarfs. Being 6'4", it doesn't take long for my back to start screaming.

Anyway, I was splitting wood while Boogie and Bentley watched—that's what they do best. As I worked up a sweat, they started panting harder. I'd stop for a drink (of water), and they would want one, too. For them it's hard work watching me swing the splitting maul. Our new puppy, Tuesday, was throwing a chunk of bark up into the air and catching it, then running in circles wanting someone to play with her.

"Not now, Tuesday," I told her. "Can't you see I'm busy?"

She tried to get Boogie to play, but all Boogie would do is show her teeth, as if to say "Can't you see I'm busy watching J.D. split wood?" Bentley wasn't into playing either.

As my pile of split wood grew, I daydreamed about having gas heat. Boogie and Bentley had grown tired of watching me and were both asleep on their backs, chasing rabbits or whatever it is dogs dream about. But where was Tuesday? I put the splitting maul down and walked to the front yard, calling her. This, of course, woke the other two dogs, and they followed me. Ah, there she was, over by the gate into the orchard, still playing with her piece of bark.

Wait a minute. That didn't look like a piece of bark. With my sweat-streaked glasses, I couldn't see very clearly. As Tuesday flung whatever it was she had into the air, I hollered at her to sit, which she did immediately (all my training was paying off). I could then see what had been in her mouth. My God, it was our pet rooster, Louie. I ran over to the poor old bird, thinking "What a way to go!" Louie had come with the place when we bought it, a dwarf bantie rooster that our tenants had gotten for food for their anaconda snake. But Louie escaped his fate. He also has survived two dog attacks over the eight years we've been here. He's always had the run of the place—he's the King of the Hill.

I picked him up. His body was wet from head to tail. He was alive, but in shock and stiff as a board. I couldn't find any puncture marks on the old boy, so I stuck him in my shirt with his head sticking out, hoping to warm him up. Boogie and Bentley knew this was not good. Old Louie was their pal. They were both sniffing his body and whining. I had a stern talk with Tuesday. I think the word "NO" was imbedded in her brain after that.

We all went to the porch where I pulled up the rocker and started talking to Louie, telling him he was going to be okay. The dogs all had their heads on my leg looking at Louis. Finally there was a little movement, so I took him out to the chicken coop to get him a shot of water. As soon as I sat him on the roost, he let go with one of the loudest screams I've ever heard from such a small critter. All twenty-nine hens and six ducks came running in from the orchard to the coop as Louie kept up his screaming (I guess he was coming out of shock and thought Tuesday still had him). I was beginning to wonder if he was going to be traumatized permanently from all of this, when he climbed into one of the nest boxes, stuck his head in a corner, and wouldn't come out.

So I left him there and went back to the wood pile. I checked up on him a few hours later, and he was out in the orchard with his ladies, doing just fine. Nothing like a good woman to make you feel better--having twenty-nine of them must really be something!

To date Tuesday has not tried to use Louis like a Frisbee again. But poor old Louie had more trauma when another rooster showed up here a few weeks later—however, that's another story.

Louie R. Shupe, the mighty rooster. We sure miss him.

There Goes the Cookie Jar

We've been having a bit of chaos at our home of late. Our Australian Shepherd, Bentley, and our new Border Collie pup, Tuesday, get along fine. Bentley gets all the exercise he needs just trying to keep up with Tuesday, or maybe trying to get away from her for a little peace and quiet. The only place Tuesday leaves Bentley alone is his bed. So that's where he tries to spend a lot of his time these days.

On the other hand, our other Australian Shepherd, Boogie, won't have anything to do with Tuesday, or, as she sees it, that other woman who has come into our lives. After all, having to share me with my wife, Sioux, is bad enough.

For example, Sioux (who works in San Francisco at the V.A. Hospital) comes home for her days off, and Boogie doesn't understand why she must give up her spot on our bed so Sioux can have it. When Sioux tells her to get off the bed, Boogie looks at me with her sad eyes, saying, "Can she clean your ears better than I can?"

Needless to say, Boogie, who wants to be the one-and-only, is so put out with more competition from Tuesday that she is doing things that she's never done before to get attention. Now, you folks with kids know this story—jealousy between siblings. Me, I had minor surgery (it seemed major to me) years ago so I wouldn't have to deal with those kinds of things. I didn't realize I'd get some of it anyway through my dogs.

Boogie learned how to open the cabinet door leading to our trash sack, and she'd then proceed to string trash all through the house. Then she'd put herself in her corner. (Each dog has a corner they get sent to when they are naughty.) I changed the latch on the door so she hasn't been able to open it since. No matter, she started pulling out the bread drawer and cleaning out our bread supply. After a few loaves and more time spent in her corner, we moved our bread to a storage place on the counter.

I thought I had everything secured. Wrong! I came home one afternoon just after Sioux got home from San Francisco. As she was coming out of the house, I ran to her and planted a nice big lip lock on her (she'd been gone for eight days). She looked up at me and said, "Honey, I've got bad news for you." She wasn't gentle with it either. "Your daughter Boogie broke your cowboy cookie jar."

No, not my cowboy cookie jar! I love that piece. Every time I lifted the pottery hat to get a cookie to dunk in my milk, I would think of the Christmas that Sioux gave it to me. I started to hope that this was a sick joke, but no such luck. When I entered the kitchen, there it lay, my smiling cowboy cookie jar with his shattered cowboy hat. How did this happen? Well, it appears that Boogie got up on the counter (jumped, used a chair, God only knows, but there was no need to dust for paw prints) and pushed my cookie jar over the edge. Boogie then proceeded to eat all the cookies that Sioux's mom had made for me.

And where was Boogie at that point? Where else but in her corner, way back under the stairs where I couldn't reach her. I know she was saying, "Bring any more women into this house and see what happens!"

I think I'm gonna get a combination safe to store my cookies in, and then we'll see if Boogie can learn safe-cracking.

Spandex Madness or Zipper Lipped?

Twice this past summer I've had very serious close calls with spandex-clad bicyclists on Highway 238. They act like the highway was built just for them. These comically costumed anorexic-looking cyclists love to ride two and three abreast through our many shoulderless blind curves, flapping their jaws, oblivious to the world. I had to hit the gravel both times (luckily there were no mailboxes in my way) to keep from slamming the other car that had to swing out into my lane to keep from hitting these clowns who were riding side by side through a blind curve. Then these bozos had the gall to glare at me like it was my fault that I was pelting them with the gravel kicked up from my tires. As I looked at their vacant eyes while sliding past them, I was sure the little wind spoilers on their helmets had sucked out what small pea brains they had and cast them to the wind. Who among us with a brain would ride a bicycle in such a manner?

Speaking of brains, where in the world did these goofy-looking outfits come from? These bicyclists look like they're from a heavy metal rock-and-roll band strongly influenced by Liberace. Maybe they have a death wish. I don't know. What I do know is that anybody dressed in pink, green, and yellow spandex, with stupid little advertisements plastered all over their bodies, gloves without fingers, shoes with cleats, and helmets with fins and air holes that look like a 1959 Cadillac, surely isn't playing with a full deck—you know, a couple of quarts shy of full. Of course, I once wore stupid-looking things like Nehru jackets, Madras pants, and psychedelic paisley capes. (I miss my capes).

My three dogs also have a bone to chew with these "I want to be a spot on the road" thrill-seekers. Boogie was having a very enjoyable ride with her head out the window, catching bugs in her teeth, when I had to take evasive action to avoid a crash with one of these pink flamingo cock-a-doodle-doo bird brains. Poor Boogie was thrown to the truck floor while her head was still between the window and the door jam. Bentley, who was riding in the back seat (extended cab pick-up) was thrown to the front seat and onto the floor where I had a bag of groceries. By then I was smoking mad. I now had a bag of crushed chips completely worthless for scooping up bean dip, a loaf of bread that looked like an old beat-up accordion, and peach juice oozing all over my new *National Enquirer* and *Soldier of Fortune* magazines.

Little Tuesday pretty much stayed in place, but with dog drool hanging from her lip. I knew she was close to being car sick (she is no fun at an amusement park). After my defensive footwork, we managed to get back safely on the roadway. Then there was a sickening sound from where Tuesday sat, and the truck was quickly permeated with the smell of you-know-what.

Now, I know that if I had had my dogs strapped into car seats or doggie seats none of this would have happened. But if these bubble-brained goofballs had been bicycling single-file, and to the far side of the lane, this story wouldn't have had to be written. After all, if we dance together on one of these curves, my truck can be fixed much more easily than a bicyclist's body, and I would be rather steamed if I had to repaint my new truck.

On the other hand, bicyclists have had their share of close calls with fat-headed, rubber-brained, zipper-lipped motorists. Let's *all* think "safety first" when we're traveling the highways.

Bentley and Boogie with giant pumpkins from our garden, 1996

Biker Chicks or Yellow Snow

Sioux and I have divvied up the household chores in our twenty-first-century home. Sioux is the cook, and what a great cook she is! Her super stuffed salmon, zany zucchini chocolate chip cake, or her beautiful beet bouquet make my mouth water just writing this. I, on the other hand, can barely open a can of tomato soup. I know, people are always telling me, "J.D. you can learn to cook." Ha! If you like your burgers raw or burnt, then I've mastered the art of cooking. But I am one of those guys who is cooking-challenged. It has taken me years of burning water to get to where I am today. I'm not a total loser in the kitchen, though. I do wash a mean pan.

Doing the laundry is one of the chores for this twenty-first-century man. My preferred choice in washing machines is a Maytag at any local laundromat. The idea of feeding a washing machine at home every other day would leave me on the spin cycle. However, I can go to the laundromat twice a month, fill up eight to twelve washing machines and dryers and, presto, two hours later I'm on my way home in the same amount of time it would take to finish one load of clothes at home.

I find the atmosphere very interesting at laundromats. The mixture of people runs from characters from a Harlequin romance novel to a Stephen King bestseller. I used to patronize a laundromat that was used by biker chicks. You know the type--leather and lace. Pretty, but "Don't mess with me, I'm tough. I could slit your throat with my little fingernail."

Once when I was folding my wash at the bikermat, I struck up a conversation with the woman across the folding table from me. She had a couple of interesting tattoos on her right arm leading down to a cast on her wrist. I asked her what had happened to her arm. She flashed a lovely smile (she had all of her teeth) and told me how this no good **** girl had tried to hustle up her old man last Saturday and that she broke her wrist while hammering home a lesson to this hussy. She shadowed-boxed to show me how she taught the lesson. I was very impressed.

Sioux was down in San Francisco working at the V.A. Hospital, so I didn't have much of her laundry with me. In fact, the only clothing with a feminine touch was her underwear. As I started to fold her undies, the biker chick took one look at them, and then at me, and said in a loud voice so everybody in the laundromat could hear, "So you're one of them!" I stood there holding Sioux's underwear as the whole place looked at me. I could feel my face turning red as she gathered her clothes and moved to another table. I believed I knew what she meant, and the looks I received from the other women told me that they knew it, too. After that humiliating experience I started using a different laundromat.

You know, you can reminisce about things while putting clothes in the laundry. Like the time I was sticking this particular towel in the wash, I thought of the night Sioux used it to dry off our Border Collie, Tuesday.

Sioux was in the hot tub asleep when--you guessed it—Tuesday decided to join her. Ever since we got Tuesday a little over a year ago, she's been interested in the spa. She licks at the water and puts her front paws in, with a look that says, "Please, can I come in?" So she finally invited herself to do just that. She swam over to Sioux and started biting at one of the water jets. Sioux was trying to get Tuesday out of the spa, but by now, our other two dogs wanted to join in the fun. Sioux had her hands full, but she convinced Boogie and Bentley not to jump in, no matter how much their paws or backs ached. Of course, I was in bed fast asleep and missed the whole show until a wet Tuesday jumped in bed with me. Arghh!

The last time I was at the laundromat, my thoughts were on the dirty rat who was responsible for the dye in my light brown shirt. I've washed this shirt many times over the three years I've owned it, so I thought I could throw it in with my light-colored clothes and the few whites that I had. I could have screamed when I pulled it out of the wash. In fact, I did scream. I jumped around like a wounded animal. By God, I was in the middle of a nuclear meltdown. All of the women in the laundromat had their eyes on me, as I held out my white t-shirts that now were the color mentioned in Frank Zappa's song, "Don't eat the yellow snow; that's where the huskies go." When my blood pressure finally started to drop, I could see the pitying looks on the faces of the women who were watching me. I knew they were thinking, "What a loser this guy is. He doesn't even know that you wash your whites separately. I bet he can't cook either. What an airhead."

My eyes were pleading, "It's not my fault. It's the person with the llama pellets for brains who uses this cheap dye in my shirt just to save a few cents." I could tell by their sniggers that they weren't buying it. As they shook their heads, it was obvious they thought I couldn't wash and chew gum at the same time.

As I placed my yellowed whites in the dryer, I was plotting the demise of those responsible for the cheap dye in my shirt—and for my disgrace in front of these ladies. After all, aren't we a society of people who think, "It's not my fault. I'm not responsible for my actions." No sir, it's always someone else who is to blame.

The Big Stink or Trail Fees

I heard a story on the news today about how we taxpayers funded the tab for a study on flatulence. It seems a doc at the V.A. Hospital in Minneapolis was given tax dollars to see what causes the passing of gas (better known as farts) to stink. If they had asked me, I could have told them for free—in my case, bean burritos (especially a bean burrito supreme). Tell me, is there anybody who really cares what makes a fart stink?

When it comes to the big stinky, most guys still show a touch of adolescence. They'll make remarks like "Good God, did you die?" or "I'm glad I don't do *your* laundry." Now, most women never do it in public--what they refer to as "I did a fluffy." But for guys, if you're the perpetrator, you will smile and blame it on the person seated next to you, as all the windows go down. If you're on a bus, it's a great way to get people to move, so you'll have lots of leg room.

Next I'm sure the government will want to know why some farts burn better than others—for alternative fuel sources, of course.

Anyway, speaking of flatulence, what is our country coming to, now that the government wants to charge trail fees on our public lands? Whoever came up with this idea surely had a big stinky that misfired and settled in his other brain. If we have enough money to study the 'Great Fart Question," why does the government need to raise money from trail fees? It is utter nonsense to charge a family to walk in the woods, sit by a stream, or daydream in a meadow.

I know it takes money to maintain the great outdoors, but excuse me, the tens of millions of people who use our parks, trails, and rivers every year already pay through the nose with the tax dollars that are squeezed out of them every year. If that isn't enough to cover the bill, then use the money we waste every year on wars or foreign aid or bridges to nowhere. That would cover the trail fees forever.

Why is it that the things taxpayers use the most—roadways, parks, etc.—always seem to be short on maintenance money? Now we will be seeing more uniforms with badges (paid for by your trail fees) in the woods. They'll be writing citations to those families whose paperwork is not in order.

I smell a big stink in the air, and it's not from the V.A. Hospital Fart Study. It's called trail fees. I, for one, will not be paying this legalized shakedown fee to those in Washington DC who can't even balance a checkbook. They're in overdraft and I refuse to bail them out!

Tuesday, Bees, and the County

Sitting in a rocker on our front porch, I'm just amazed when I look out on our gardens. The lupines, poppies, iris, and columbine are all in bloom by the hundreds. The reds, blues, purples, yellows, oranges, and pinks make it look like a rainbow fell into our yard.

Yes, this year's spring rain has given us a glorious garden. I know many folks didn't care for our wet, cloudy weather, but, me, I loved it. It must be my English and Scottish bloodlines. You have to remember the worst weather day in the Applegate is better than the best day in, say, Detroit or Indianapolis. I know—I've seen both.

Whenever Sioux or I take a stroll through the garden, Boogie, Bentley, and Tuesday follow. They're real good about staying on the walkways and out of the flowerbeds. However, Tuesday does have one bad habit on these walks. She loves to bite at the honeybees, bumblebees, or any other flying insect that's working the flowers along the pathway.

Now, I'm a slow learner, not much brighter than a lug nut, but I can guarantee that I'd only have to get stung once or twice (okay, maybe three times) to be broken of such an addiction. Not Tuesday. A sting or a bite just makes her more determined to snap their little heads off in mid-flight. Maybe this goes back to her puppyhood. I don't know; should I have given her more doggie treats? I mean, she won't back down from even yellow jackets or wasps. This could be a real problem if killer bees ever get this far north.

Old Boogie and Bentley always look at me when Tuesday is playing Dirty Harry with an expression that says: "We are not going to play 'bite the head off the bee.' It's just not going to happen. Now, if you want to play ball or fetch the stick, we're game, but 'rip the wings from a hornet'—no way." I always point out that I never tell Tuesday to "bite the bees." I don't want her to turn a live one loose on me.

Golly, there are plenty of ways, as it is, to get stung in life without encouraging a bee attack. Think of the times you may have been stung over the years by more than a wayward bee. Let's see--there's a bad check, or a bum car, or a poor investment, or—I know!—a bad land deal, like when the county auctioned off the parking lot to the Applegate Park. Now that the Park is closed, the summer gathering place for Applegators may be history. A swarm of three county commissioners stung the whole community, and that has raised one heck of a welt. Here, Tuesday!!

Little Miss Tuesday feeling much better the day after her midnight emergency veterinarian run.

Summer Cookin' or Hosin' Down the Kitchen

For those of you who love the heat, I hope you enjoyed your summer. But for heat wimps like me, it was hard to find any relief (I wish I had a walk-in cooler to hang out in). I had a tough time battling Boogie, Bentley, and

Tuesday for a spot in front of my fan. By the way the three dogs act, you would think it was *their* fan.

Come early afternoon it would be too hot for me to work in the garden, so I'd stretch out in front of the fan. I would block out the rattle and hum of the fan from my ears and drift off to sleep with the cool air blowing on me. On entering dreamland, I found myself standing next to a cold, frothing waterfall. I was shrouded in a cool mist with my favorite drink in hand, lying back in an oh-so-comfy recliner.

Then, all at once, my dream had a dramatic change. I was standing on a sand dune in some godforsaken place under a melting sun that looked like a welder's ark. My lips were chapped and blistered, and my bare feet were on fire in the sand. I woke up in a soaking sweat with Boogie lying on my feet. Bentley and Tuesday also were at my feet, blocking any and all airflow from my fan. The dogs' long hair was blowing gently in the air, while mine was plastered to my head with sweat. I told the three of them to move away from the fan-- better yet, get off the bed. All three dogs just looked at me, yawned, and turned over. "Hey, who pays the power bill here?" But none of them cared.

I got up and called my outlaw buddy (a County Commissioner now—who would have ever guessed?), the Honorable Al "El Supremo" McLeod in Moab, Utah. I was whining and sniffling about our 107 degree heat when Al told me to take it like a man. He was dealing fine at 118 degrees. Maybe 107 wasn't so bad after all.

Two of my long-time friends (also escapees from Utah), Bill and Kris Davis, came up from Stockton, California, for a visit. They informed me it was much cooler here than in Stockton. Bill and Kris had their two very large collies with them--Gala and Pukka. Pukka was recovering from a bad trip on fly bait, so she was moving a little slower than normal, but I can tell you, with five dogs underfoot it didn't matter how slow one dog moved. I thought I was living in the Jackson County dog pound.

The dogs all got along fairly well, as well as most cousins do at family reunions or funerals. Tuesday wound up in her corner more than a couple of times for wanting to be Queen of the Hill. She was very jealous when Bentley (the only male) would try to play with Pukka in the pasture.

Tuesday would bite Bentley on the back leg (that's a Border collie for you) and trip him up. Gala would then stand around and bark, while Boogie lay in the grass paying no one any mind at all. She was above all that. (Isn't it kind of hard keeping straight which dog is who? But that's how it goes when you're living in a kennel.)

Bill was here to give a class on journalism law (he teaches journalism at a college in Stockton) to the Applegate Partnership and anyone else who wanted to participate. The morning of the class I was up early (well, kind of early, considering the reminiscing party we had the night before). I set up a few sprinklers around the outside of the house, then went out to the vegetable garden to do some hand-watering. I was enjoying the cool, quiet morning that was still less than ninety degrees. I looked at my watch and saw we needed to head off to class.

As I walked to the house I noticed water running down the side of it. Funny, I had the sprinkler facing away from the house. As I got closer, I let out a shriek that could be heard down to the Applegate Store. The sprinkler was pointed right into our screen door, straight into the kitchen. There was Pukka going "Oh dum-de-dum-de-dum, isn't it great to play with a sprinkler?" Bentley, who was next to me, started shaking all over. I knew he was saying "This isn't good, but I had nothing to do with it." Tuesday thought this would be a great time to play ball. Boogie looked at me with an expression that said, "What do you expect? Aren't these collies from Stockton?" Gala was just standing around barking at all the excitement.

I turned the water off and entered the kitchen. The scene wasn't what I had in mind when I thought about an indoor pool. Water was dripping off the counter, the walls, the windows (inside and out) and was deep on the kitchen floor. I felt like I had survived the great New Year's flood of '97, only to get washed out by a collie.

Kris took the broom, and I got the mop, and we started the clean-up. Bill, who missed all the excitement because he was in the shower, walked into the kitchen and thought it strange I was being domestic when it was time to leave for class. It was kindly, even politely, pointed out to him that his dog had decided to hose down the kitchen. I asked him if he thought insurance from the college covered dog damages. I'm sure we'll have to raze the whole house and build again. I told him I'm sure FEMA wouldn't cover a one-house flash flood caused by Pukka. As I mopped and Kris swept we found that the floor wasn't ruined but was now sparkling clean. Maybe this wasn't so bad. When Sioux got home from San Francisco she'd be *so* impressed with my cleaning abilities.

Pukka got her own corner for when she's bad, and Bill's class came off without a hitch. In fact, I even took notes, more pages of notes than I had taken in the last two years of high school (although the paper I was using now was only 2"x3").

Whack-a-Booms or Latte Futures

What to write about for this issue of the *Applegator*? Road hunting might be good; it's that time of year again. But I think I'll write about tourism—that oversold savior for downward spiraling communities of the West.

I do know a little about this topic. My old hometown of Moab, Utah, went for the tourism gold when the last uranium mine shut down. The same government geniuses that advised us (from a safe distance) that we get into uranium mining were now advising downsizing our paychecks from $200 a day (1983 dollars) to $40 a day (1998 dollars), and buying into latte futures and chainsaw sculpture.

The result of the tourism trade was, for most people, not the predicted explosion in the local economy, but a first-name familiarity with the local collection agency personnel. They also needed a suicide prevention hotline number to post over grease-encrusted 911 emergency numbers tacked on kitchen cabinet doors throughout town. Yes sir, pawnshop prosperity sure sounds good to me.

How will you know a tourist when you see one? They're often found camping in flocks, or stopped on a blind curve in clusters doing a fifty-minute video of two waddling, oversized, pre-diabetic chipmunks eating only the red M&Ms. You can find them wearing those wild pink and yellow plaid Bermuda shorts, while their white tube socks with no elastic sag down around their genuine

Chinese-made flip-flops, and sporting an artistically highlighted mustard-and-relish-stained shirt that reads "Just say No to Crack," as they're bent *way* over peering down the blowhole at Old Faithful hollering, "Dear, it's five minutes past the time this thang is supposed to blow, and I don't see nothin'." Then there are the more challenging conversations one can have with tourists that run along the lines of "Where's the McDonalds?" or "Do you have a KOA camp?" or "Why is there no toilet paper in this here outhouse?"

Within the tourist species there is a sub-species known as the groover. Staunch environmentalists all, they believe that Nature is sacred, at least until their dividend check is diminished by pro-environmental policy. Hard to believe but true; they've cornered the market on reality impairment, especially as it pertains to other peoples' livelihoods. The devoted worshipers of the latest doodah parade of useless gizmo toys await the "Harmonic Convergence," crystals in hand, sitting in their new Lincoln Navigators, while dispensing advice from on high to the rest of us "unwashed masses."

Yes, tourism has so much to offer. Why wouldn't a family, holding down part-time jobs, polishing bowling balls, making double cappuccinos, and selling tour maps showing their once-favorite fishing hole, not be overjoyed by such glorious opportunities to serve?

Remember, it costs money to staff and equip a Search & Rescue team, so we locals will get to pay more taxes. There is sure to be some whack-a-boom from New Jersey who will try to shove a bear behind the wheel of the family minivan for a great photo op. His wife will ask, "Honey, do you think this is a good idea?" moments before the bear attacks. Isn't natural selection great? But this will cost us big bucks. The county will be sued for not having signs posted and stickers on the behinds of all the bears of southern Oregon warning tourists of such potential dangers. The courts will say, "Tourists can't be held at fault, he/she left their gray matter (known to the rest of us as a brain) at home on the coffee table or in the deep freeze."

I don't dislike tourists; I've been a tourist. I think we've all been tourists on occasion. Just think of some of the stupid things you've said or done as a tourist. Now ask yourself, is this the industry you would want to work in or the people you would want to be surrounded by for 365 days a year? A little tourism is okay—just so it's somewhere else!

A Charmed Life, But No Fruitful Eggs

An era has passed here at Rocky Thistle Ranch. The great Louie R. Shupe has passed on. Who was Louie, you ask? Well, his name has appeared in this column several times over the years. The mighty Louie, as many folks referred to him, was a one-and-a-half pound raging terror (in his own mind).

At eleven years of age this bantam rooster was still ruling the roost--although for the past few months, old Louie hit the roost long before his girls retired for the night. His once beautiful red and iridescent green feathers with the black and white speckles just didn't shine as they used to. I knew the old boy's days were numbered.

Louie came with the place when Sioux and I bought our piece of paradise. We had rented it out for awhile before moving in, and the folks we rented to had a seventeen-foot pet boa constrictor (we didn't know this), and Louie was to be dinner for Mr. Snake. Louis escaped his fate by making a jail (or cage) break. When we moved in, he was running wild around the place. If you got within twenty feet of him, he was off in a flash of red feathers.

Louie roosted in the tops of the lilac bushes the first winter we were here. We had a heavy wet snow one night that bent the lilacs halfway to the ground. I was able to retrieve Louie, with three inches of wet snow on his back, and move him to the barn.

After that Louie and I became fast friends. When Sioux and I worked around the place, he'd hang out with us and demand that we hand-feed him fresh-dug earthworms. He became pals with our Australian Shepherd, Boogie. When Boogie had her pups, she let Louie hang out with them. The pup we kept, Bentley, always thought Louie was his little brother.

Louie developed a taste for cat food. He ate with our cats on the outside window ledge looking into the kitchen. If the cat bowl was empty, he'd peck on the window to let us know. I was never able to enter him in the crowing contest in Rogue River because Louie had such a pathetic, stupid crow. In fact, it was downright embarrassing. But he must have thought it was great, as he strutted around crowing all day.

With our good friend Keith Boyle's expert hands, we put up a six-sided chicken coop with electricity and running water that became known as "Louie's Palace." We ordered two dozen hens to go along with the palace, because what good is a rooster without hens?

Being as how Louie was so small and the hens were so big, we rarely had a fruitful egg. So we got a couple of other roosters (large ones), but Louie so terrorized them they stayed hidden in the corners of the chicken yard. The nine-inch-tall Louie would then run around cackling this sound that you would swear was from some madman locked away in a dungeon. So the new roosters went to the freezer and Louie was as happy as a sheik with his harem.

We free-ranged our chickens in the orchard, which allowed Louie to go wherever he wanted. He fit through the fence easily, which set him up for three different dog attacks, one of which I wrote about in this column, when Sioux brought home a lost Border Collie that she named Tuesday. That day Louie became a red tennis ball for Tuesday, as she threw him up into the air and caught him over and over again. Louie survived, and Tuesday learned that he wasn't a toy. Another time a friend's dog gave chase to Louie, but only got tail feathers for his effort. Across the road and up the hillside ran Louie. I searched for him, shaking a can of dry cat food, but couldn't find him. After a few days we gave him up for lost. I was sure a raccoon had chowed him down. Nope, one morning he was back knocking at the kitchen window, wanting some cat food. Then he was off to see his girls. I guess you can tell that Louie led a charmed life.

He truly entertained us and anyone else who made his acquaintance. You might think that this is a long obituary for a rooster, but I tell you, he wasn't just any old rooster--he was Louie R. Shupe!

Louie trying to work his way through the puppies for some chow with Mama Boogie looking on, 1991

Belt Buckles Bigger Than Heads, or Long-term Planning

It was 3:27 a.m. when I looked at the alarm clock. Great, I'd tossed and turned for two hours already. I closed my eyes and squeezed my eyelids real tight, pulled the blankets up over my head, but sleep wouldn't come. I wanted to wake up Sioux and ask her if she'd like to go for a middle-of-the-night ride, but she was in San Francisco at her nursing job.

So I lay there, listening to Boogie, Bentley, and Tuesday snore, snort, and make that little cry that dogs do in their sleep. I wondered if all three of them were chasing the same squirrel. So just for a reaction I said, "Did you hear that?" All at once they were dancing around ready to give chase. Boogie started to whine and then bark. I told her to relax, that I was just monkeying with them. Then they all gave me a look that said, "You got us up for this? You've got a sick mind."

In the dark, I headed out to the living room, stubbing my toe on Tuesday's gnawed knucklebone. I said a few censored words as I pulled the rocker up in front of our new woodstove. Many of our friends are pleased that we got it. They comment on how nice it is to stop by for a visit without having to wear three layers of woolen clothing, battery-operated heat socks, insulated arctic boots, and a ski mask made out of some space-age heat-inducing material. Yes sir, it's now many degrees above thirty-two in this house. The dogs each went to their favorite spot to stretch out and get back to their doggie dream world.

While staring at the fire, I noticed that it was so quiet that if I really strained my eardrums (I should be deaf from some of the rock bands I've played in), I could hear Thompson Creek rushing over the rocks with its magical rhythmic song. Then I started to wonder how long it would take that water I had just heard to make its way to the Applegate River and then on down to the Rogue River and finally to the Pacific Ocean?

Since I've been involved in stream side (riparian area) restoration, either first hand or from articles in the *Applegator*, I'm always visually checking the condition of the streams I see. I thought back to our recent vacation to Texas to see my parents. On our first day's drive we pulled up to a signal light, and I looked out at a construction zone where a sign informed us that it was the future site of another architecturally demeaning mini-mall and condominium development. There was a man just a few feet away who was as thin as cellophane. He had a belt buckle bigger than his head, a head that sported a yellow hard hat. I was amazed he could walk around the muddy area in his pointy-toed, high-heeled boots (definitely not steel-toed), but then he was just leaning on a shovel, with cigarette smoke rolling around a ruddy face, staring at heavy equipment running up, down, across, and through a creek as far as the eye could see. The water ran thick with mud, as there were no barriers of any kind set up to catch it. The developer *had* left some oaks that were small by Oregon standards, but nice trees nevertheless.

On another day, we passed a creek the size of the Little Applegate River that had a new fifteen-foot-high dam with no fish passages anywhere. The dam made a very nice-looking waterfall that dropped into a great swimming hole. There were many high-priced houses being built all along this creek. I wondered, "What would happen if I built a dam like that on Thompson Creek?" I would probably get on a first-name basis with some guy named Bubba up in Pendleton State Prison.

Now, I know the Texas hill country doesn't have salmon or steelhead runs, but I guarantee they'll wind up with some sort of sucker fish or minnow that most folks have never heard of nor care about, that will become threatened or endangered, and then the wars will start. It seems to me that with everything that is known about riparian areas and fish nowadays, folks would do some serious long-term planning. But that seems never to happen until there is a problem.

This indicates to me that, overall, the Applegate is light years ahead of many other places in our country. We have many fine folks working on riparian restoration and trying to solve fish-passage problems. I just wish we didn't have to have rules and regulations by the semi-load for a lot of things that should be just plain old common sense.

The Reports of My Death Are Greatly Exaggerated

I knew something was wrong when the thumping of my heart was louder than the jake-brake on a fully loaded log truck running down Thompson Creek Road. I found myself in a fetal position, doubled up on the couch. When I couldn't take a breath I knew that I was having the Big One. My sweet bride, Sioux, was in San Francisco and about to start one of the longest nights of her life, driving home at 1:00 a.m. after twelve hours of work, not knowing what was going on with me.

I called my neighbors, Linda and Bob Fischer. Linda, being used to my mumbling, easily figured out it was me on the other end of the phone. She replied, "J.D., do you need some help?" I managed to get out another moan, and they were over to my house in a flash. They didn't attempt a diagnosis, but just shoved me into their shiny new red pick-up truck as best they could and headed for Rogue Valley Medical Center.

Bob, being an ex-motorcop, knew how to shave at least eight miles off Highway 238. I never knew the road was so straight. I was doing the best I could to keep my earlier dinner down. Bob must have sensed this, as he imagined himself on his motorcycle (the Blue Knight is back) and buzzed me quickly and safely to the emergency room. Linda (it's nice to have angels around) held my head as level as possible so I wouldn't feel the curves so much. Her actions also helped save the interior of their truck.

By the time we arrived at the emergency room, I thought it was all over. I had never been in such pain *in my life,* and I have experienced pain before. The medics ran all their different tests. It was after the chest x-ray that they came to the conclusion that it was not my heart, but rather my stomach that was in a politically incorrect position. It had herniated up through my diaphragm and was pushing against my heart and lung.

The doctor gave me two choices: I could have surgery, or I could die. I opted for the first choice. I was wheeled into the waiting line for a surgery room. (It was a busy night for serious medical work). When the big moment arrived, and I was rolled into the operating room, classical music was blasting from the loudspeakers. Now, my first choice in music would have been "Highway to Hell" or "Sin City" by AC/DC, but my doctor later told me when I went under the knife that he was playing jazz music. When I woke up in my room, I was minus a spleen, radically rearranged internally, and held together with thirty-nine staples down my belly.

Ten days later, Sioux brought me home. The dogs were glad to see me, and expressed it by jumping, dancing, and barking as I entered the house. Even though Sioux had brought Boogie and Bentley up to see me at the hospital, they acted like I had been gone forever. Little Tuesday now will not leave my side.

You are probably saying to yourself, "Where is this going?" Well, it's to say what a great community we have here. While I was in the hospital with Sioux at my bedside several friends cleaned the house and did the laundry. After I came home, fourteen people showed up here at the house with their own wheelbarrows and shovels to move three truckloads of manure to the garden, clean out the chicken coop, and move the many bags of wet leaves Sioux and I had collected throughout the winter. This group did all the heavy stuff I won't be able to do for months. Dozens of other folks have offered to help around the place. All I have to do is ask.

All of this has taught me that community, partnerships, and friends are all one and the same: folks pulling together to help solve problems. Thanks to all.

Stiff Neck or"I Paid For This..."

Flying used to be a pleasurable experience. Now it's on a par with medieval torture. Airline seats have got to be a first cousin to the Rack. Definitely the same inventor. As I looked around the airplane on my flight from San Antonio, I could see people struggling to ease themselves into some position that might resemble comfort. No way. You're on an airplane, and comfort is not in an airline's vocabulary (at least not the one I was flying on).

Folks tell me, "You're 6'4"—you're just too big for the seats." But I weigh less than 200 pounds. Well, maybe right around 200. Hey, that's not *big*. Big was the guy in front of me. Jumbo didn't quite describe him. As soon as we were airborne, back came his seat, forcing my knees to retract into my hip sockets. I thought, "I'm paying for this treatment." Fortunately for my insurance man and bail bond man, when I asked the gentleman he pulled his seat up a notch or two. I was enjoying my couple of inches of leg freedom when the beverage cart ran into my right leg. With a damaged leg, hurt knees, and a stiff neck like I hadn't felt in years, my stress level was giving me a powerful thirst. So I ordered my drink of choice, hoping to numb my pain.

I barely made my connecting flight in Denver—where I was one of the last to board my flight to Los Angeles. I wasn't looking forward to the few hours that lay ahead, chained in a seat designed by a midget sadist. I tried to adjust my microscopic airflow valve, but I didn't get much air. Great! Nothing to breathe except jet exhaust fumes. Why don't they add some scented fragrance, such as swamp gas or compost? Even the old Jacksonville dump scent would be better than what I was breathing. I was wiggling around worse than a two-year-old when our pilot informed us that there was a valve stuck in the open position, and it had to be closed for us to fly.

"Nothing to worry about," he said. "A mechanic will wire it shut. Then we'll be on our way." I thought, "They're wiring this valve shut. Are they using baling wire? This isn't good." Then the pilot said to just sit back and relax. That was easy for him to say. He obviously had a better seat than I did. Besides, I was thinking of all the things I've used baling wire on, such as the muffler on my '59 Oldsmobile and the rear bumper of my old rusted '63 VW. But airplane parts are for flying at 25,000 feet. I was sure the airline uses a higher grade of wire, right?

I started to feel sweat running down my brow, and I was getting that closed-in feeling called claustrophobia. This was embarrassing because I used to work in uranium mines 1,600 feet underground. I closed my eyes and tried to imagine more favorable surroundings--a Turkish prison, Siberia; Cleveland, Ohio. Thank God that worked. The urge to run screaming off the plane had passed as we finally lifted off an hour and fifteen minutes late.

The flight attendant handed out headsets so we could hear the entertainment on the mini-monitor screens. If you're one of the folks who like a TV screen built into your wristwatch, you'd love that screen. I put my headset on, but it kept slipping off my ears. It's not like I'm new to headsets. I've worn them in many recording studios and, of course, on other flights. However, you'd have to be a Conehead or Mr. Zippy to keep this set on. I asked for and got another set. I was finally hooked up, ready to be entertained, and a commercial began about how this airline does all it can to make your flight enjoyable. I could guarantee you that the guy on the screen didn't fly in the "head 'em up—move 'em out" section of the airplane that I was on. I'll bet he's never seen this section of the plane where it takes an electric cattle prod to crowd everybody into his or her seating areas. Oh man, was my neck stiff. Didn't they used to show movies on airline flights? Seems they've now "upgraded" to the worst of the worst TV sitcoms complete with TV commercials. Yes, I paid for this "fly the friendly skies" experience. I was feeling very thirsty again.

By the time I got to Los Angeles, I'd gone through all of my fast-acting antacid tablets (you ever eaten on an airplane?) and Motrin, along with whatever else I could find in my carry-on bag. As I hobbled off this "friendly sky airline," the feeling slowly came back to my legs. No way could I run, but then why bother? My flight to Medford left ten minutes ago. Not to worry, the next Medford flight had a three-hour delay posted.

So my flight (that I didn't miss) went from a three-hour delay to a five-hour delay. That's a long time to wander in LAX airport. And, of course, the same sadist who designed the seats for the airplanes also designed the seats for the airport. While wandering in and out of the airport bookstore for the hundredth time, I discovered that I had drained the last of my St. John's Wort extract. I knew I should have bought the XXXL size for this trip because I was about to discover on the flight monitor that my flight had been cancelled. Excuse me! I made a lightning-bolt dash (in slow motion) over to my loading gate, where I was told, "Yes, Mr. Rogers, the Medford flight has been cancelled. The plane couldn't get out of San Francisco." Unbelievable. I had booked the direct, non-stop flight from L.A. to Medford because the ticket agent told me that I wouldn't have to deal with the San Francisco airport or its weather problems. Now why was my direct flight airplane in San Francisco and grounded for the night?

I was told that I should go find the bags that I had checked. "Just look for all the other unhappy travelers in the baggage claim area." I noticed that about ninety percent of the travelers that night looked like they'd just been told they had some incurable terminal disease (lots of cancelled flights). My neck sure could have used a massage!

I got myself rebooked for the next morning flight to Medford and received a hotel room voucher from the ticket agent. "Thank you, thank you!" Not everyone got the treasured vouchers. I'm sure my disheveled looks, slurred speech, and head cocked at a forty-five degree angle (due to total neck muscle collapse), and my tiny eyes like red coals tipped off the agent, who probably thought I fit the profile of "cheaper to put this sputtering nuclear reactor into a hotel room than to deal with him." Good profile analysis!

After checking into my room and calling my darling wife for the third time today to fill her in on my new arrival time, I hit the hotel lounge. All right! Saturday night in LA! What, no live music? Or any music? Just a dozen or so angry Australians who had also missed their flights due to delays.

After a rugged three hours of sleep and a long shower, I still looked as hammered as the night before. Since I wasn't lucky enough (as some were) to get a food voucher, I decided to pass on the $19.95 breakfast special and head for the airport. While rechecking my bags I was told "Yes sir, Mr. Rogers. The flights are running on time." Well, if you believed that, I had some Rocky Mountain property in Sucker Hill, Iowa, that I would have loved to sell you. That's right--four more hours of delay.

After thirty-plus hours of travel, I finally arrived back in the Applegate, where my private nurse and wife, Sioux, worked on my neck. It will probably never be the same. All three of our dogs tried to get in my lap at the same time. It's nice to be loved! As for the airline—well, I'd better not say it.

Dogs, Skunks, and Public Speaking

"Man, what is it with you three dogs? Yea, yea, I know that dance you're doing—you need to go out." I looked at the alarm clock. It read 4:30 a.m., and I realized that I'd never get back to that neurotic dream I was having. Staggering out of bed, I told the dogs what good little puppies they would be if they would wait until 6:30 to wake me, but did they care?

I started thinking about how I was to be the guest speaker that night at a meeting of the Southern Oregon Small Woodlot Association (S.O.S.W.A.), and I didn't have a clue what I was going to say. I was supposed to give a run-down on myself and why I believe in the partnerships.

The dogs weren't two feet out the door when Tuesday went into a mad howling bark and tore off into the night with Bentley right behind her and Boogie bringing up the rear. I was thinking there must be a deer on the other side of our deer fence, when my eyes started watering and breathing became difficult. I must have been on a World War I battlefield covered with mustard gas in France, but no, it was a war between the dogs and an infiltrating skunk.

Tuesday gave a yelp as she took a direct hit, followed by Bentley. Boogie ran back to me foaming at the mouth, but with no skunk stench covering her. She must have been foaming from the memory of previous skunk encounters when she was sprayed. Boogie then ran into the house and headed toward her corner. She knew that chasing skunks was a no-no.

"Oh God, is this a sign of how the day is going to go?" I thought. "Maybe I had better cancel my speaking commitment for tonight." I don't do that sort of thing very often anyway. What if I got up in front of these folks and just spaced out or worse, just started drooling? By now, I'd gotten a couple of cans of tomato juice and baking soda together, as I pondered this bad omen.

I put Tuesday into the shower first. Actually she jumped in herself, followed by me. I covered her in a concoction of tomato juice and baking soda. She got a rather depressed and humiliated look, and I added to it by saying, "Why, why, why haven't you learned? Don't chase skunks!"

My mind started composing my speech as I scrubbed Tuesday down.

"Everything in life is a partnership in a sense-- marriage, family, and business. I find that by working together and setting aside one's differences, you are more apt to achieve success. Partnerships won't give you exactly what you want, but what in life will? I do know that if we don't work together, we will fall together."

I finished scrubbing Tuesday, who still smelled of skunk, dried her off, and then put Bentley in the shower. He started shaking all over (Didn't the Guess Who have a song called "Shakin' All Over?"). I didn't scold Bentley much as he was already traumatized by the whole thing. I covered him with tomato juice--an elixir that didn't seem to work-- and then returned to planning my speech.

"Hi! I'm a songwriter, editor of the Applegator, an ex-uranium miner and outlaw from Utah. I participate in the Applegate Partnership because . . ." Bentley made a break from the shower, jumping out and taking part of the shower curtain down with him. I banged my knee on the tub (I couldn't believe how much that hurt) while trying to block his escape. All 6'4" and 200 pounds of me lay sprawled out in the tub, while the fifty-pound dog proceeded to shake tomato juice into and onto everything in the bathroom. This was worse than the bad sign from the stench critter known as skunk. All this foul luck and the sun wasn't even up yet. The walls ran red, and I was thinking I didn't want to be a speaker tonight. I'd probably be electrocuted by the microphone or impale myself with a dinner fork.

I spent the next several hours cleaning the tomato juice-covered walls in the bathroom, while composing more of my speech. Let's see:

"I'm opposed to clear cuts, over story removal, and the excessive road building that has gone on in our watershed, but I use wood fiber. I live in an old log house, and I do believe in resource management, thinning from below; very, very small regeneration cuts; restoring oak woodlands, and reintroducing fire to the ecosystem. For me, the Applegate Partnership is the perfect vehicle to do this."

For the rest of the day I didn't venture out to do much of anything for fear that a bad moon might be over my shoulder. I still managed to burn myself on the wood stove. I danced around, flailing my arms and hollering like a gun-shot banshee. (The burn did take my mind off my injured knee.) I called Sioux, who was down in San Francisco at her job. I wallowed in self-pity as I relayed the story of my day to her. I asked her, since she is a nurse, if she couldn't fax me a note of excuse from my speaking commitment that night, saying how mentally deranged I was. Sioux said, "Yes, but you'll do fine, honey. I've got to go."

So off I went to the S.O.S.W.A. dinner. I managed not to wreck my truck, but I started thinking about the lunar eclipse that is to take place tonight while I'm speaking. Oh yea, that was a sign. I checked in and mingled with the crowd. I looked for the open bar, but there wasn't one—another sign.

I met the other speakers and, right off, I noticed they had written out notes for their speeches. Uh oh, maybe I should have done that, but then that might explain my 0.5 grade point average back in high school.

I was introduced and walked up to the podium. (It sure was warm up there. No microphone. Good--I wouldn't be electrocuted.) I looked out at the crowd and thought— that's what I'll say! Somehow a concoction of the above story rolled off my tongue, and no lightning bolt rained down on me from the heavens. Yep, I survived and did fine—just like my wife said I would.

Bentley—Isn't he cute? 1993

"What a Workout!" or The Here and Now

There's nothing like a good cup of coffee and toasted cinnamon-chip bread, dripping with butter, from the Great Harvest Bread Company in Medford to start the day. I polished off the last bite of toast—actually our three dogs, Boogie, Bentley, and Tuesday, got the last bites. Heck, they deserved it. All three just sat there at attention, moving only their eyes, the whole time I was eating. As I moved the bread from plate to mouth and back to plate, I would occasionally hear a whimper deep in someone's throat that seemed to say, "Please give me a bite." Of course, I always do, because they have trained me so well.

I polished off my coffee and decided that today was the day I was going to start an exercise program. No, I wasn't giving up hot cinnamon-chip bread drowned in butter; I was just going to work out more. I had to get into shape. I was going to be meeting with my old Utah outlaw buddies soon, and they are all buffed out—Chip and Dale's dudes have nothing on these guys. My outlaw buds could bench press five, maybe ten, pounds, do half a sit-up and need oxygen after one push-up. Nope, it wouldn't take me long to reach their towering figures of fitness.

I moved the furniture around in our bedroom so that I would have plenty of room for my workout. I put AC/DC "Highway to Hell" on the stereo, and started with some stomach crunches. On my first one the three dogs decided this was a new game. As I lifted my body forward I was greeted with an onslaught of kisses.

"Go away," I told them, "can't you see this is serious business?"

Next crunch--I could sure feel my stomach tightening up. Yep, I must have been toughening up already. With the third one, the dogs were back, and Tuesday decided it would be fun to stand on my chest. I doubt if she weighs more than twenty pounds, so I figured she would just add to my fitness program if I left her standing on me. I lifted up yet again, only to get a tongue-washing from all three again. I ran the dogs out of the room as AC/DC sang "No stop sign gonna slow me down." Well, it obviously wasn't going to slow down Boogie, Bentley, and Tuesday.

I decided to try some push-ups next. One—well, that wasn't too bad. Two—a green tennis ball was dropped on the back of my head by Tuesday. Obviously, she found this boring and wanted to play ball. Bentley started barking so I guess he wanted to play, too.

Three crunches and two push-ups were enough exercise for one morning. I didn't want to overdo it. Out to the hot tub I went to relax my aching muscles. What a workout!

While swimming around the hot tub, I took in the beautiful morning. I watched a pair of western tanagers fly from a Douglas fir to a black oak tree. There was a pair of mallards swimming in the creek; a chorus of songbirds filled the morning air. The sky was blue. Day lilies and delphiniums were in bloom, while the last of the peonies dropped their petals. It was just a perfect morning.

I started thinking (that's when I usually get into trouble) how folks spend so much time dwelling in the past or dreaming about the future that we just miss the here and now. There's never enough time. We race here and race there, but do we really go anywhere? We always think that some day we'll have more time to enjoy life and its many splendors such as this beautiful morning. But we don't really know how much time we've been given, so shouldn't we take a little time to enjoy each and every day? I vote yes to that.

My thoughts were broken by a splash in the water. Tuesday was looking at me over the side of the hot tub, and her tennis ball was floating towards me. She was determined to make time for what is important to *her*. So, being the well-trained human that I am, I tossed the ball for her. Besides, this is the here and now.

Shopping for Cookies

Asking "Who wants a cookie?" was a bad way for me to start the day with our dogs. All three of them took up their sitting position in front of our three-foot-high refrigerator, staring at the cookie jar that sits on top. I told them what good puppies they were. They made little whimpering noises that sounded like they were saying, "Yes, yes, we know that, now hurry up with the cookies!" I lifted the top off the jar only to find it was empty. Oh man, was I in trouble. I had forgotten to pick up some cookies the last time I was in town.

Sioux had once again suggested, "Honey, if you would write up a list before heading to town, these things wouldn't happen." I didn't tell her that I had made a list, but that I had forgotten to look at it. Anyway, now all three dogs were giving me that look that says, "What a loser. Even a pea brain should be able to remember to get more doggie cookies." Before a revolution broke out, I hollered, "Who wants to go for a ride to get some more dog cookies?" The three of them just about knocked me down, jumping and barking, as we headed out the door to the Big Blue Ram.

Bentley and Tuesday hopped in the back seat while I lifted Boogie onto her throne, the front passenger seat.

Boogie had suffered a slight stroke the week before, and she wasn't able to jump very well. Boogie also looked at me now with her head cocked at a forty-five-degree angle. I kept waiting for her to do a "Linda Blair" from the *Exorcist* with a complete rotation of her head. That made me nervous, since I blew the cookie test, so I tried not to think about Boogie starring in a remake of *The Exorcist* as we headed down Highway 238 to town.

The parking lot at the new Win Co store in Medford was packed when we arrived. I had to park in the back forty and hike in. I glanced over my shoulder at the truck, where all three dogs had their heads pushed against the side windows glaring at me. I muttered under my breath, "Okay, already, I'm hurrying."

Entering the store, I felt a panic attack coming on. There were more people than at the mall at the height of the Christmas season. Man, I hate big crowds, but I felt I had to redeem myself, so on I went through the automatic doors into the jaws of shopping madness.

We all know that some folks leave their brains at home when they go on vacation. Well, I think that applies to shopping, too. I'm surprised we haven't read in the paper: "Shopping cart rage—on aisle four (salad dressings) in such and such market—leaves 40 dead and 100 injured." Think about it: people block the whole shopping aisle with their carts or their bodies as they stare blankly at a box of cornflakes or a can of peas. People could be backed up for blocks in both directions before someone would finally say, "Excuse me, could I get by?" (rather than ramming their cart out of the way). You'd get an "I was here first, buddy" look. Your responding look would be "Yeah, well, you're going to wear this can of tamales where the sun don't shine if you don't get a move on." I'm sure those detector things you pass through as you go in and out of a store aren't really looking for merchandise that you inadvertently forgot to pay for. I think they're looking for guns, knives, steel pipe, and timing chains, so that store security can stop trouble before it starts in a traffic-jammed aisle.

Anyway, never having been in this new store, I didn't know where I was going. I passed through produce. "Excuse me, ma'am, may I get by please? Hello, could you move your cart? I'm still waiting." Maybe if stores handed out hearing aids turned up to top volume when you got your shopping cart, folks might be able to hear your plea for passage. Uh huh, no wonder she wouldn't move—bananas were fifteen cents a pound, so I snatched up two lone stragglers. I also picked up a ten-pound bag of flour for ninety-eight cents. Uh huh, they failed the Miracle Whip test—it wasn't the cheapest in the land. Where, oh where, were those doggie cookies? I witnessed two carts colliding head-on in front of the meat freezer, where some old geezer had loaded about 100 pounds of hamburger into his cart. It looked to me like a lifetime supply for this old guy. The carts involved in the accident wobbled on down the aisle. In the dairy section traffic came to a complete stop—a mighty cart logjam. I couldn't back up or move sideways. As I noticed that my breathing had started to become more difficult, I contemplated leaving my cart and making a run for it, but I realized I had to find those doggie cookies.

Finally, the carts started moving again, and I decided to do the worst of the worst, the most unmanly thing a guy can do—ask a friendly clerk for directions. Sioux would have been very proud of me, and the dogs would have been very pleased, but, me, I felt humiliated, a failure and, yes, a loser. It was the only thing I could think of doing to keep from losing my mind. (Yes, I realize there are those of you who think I have already lost it.) Anyway, I was picturing an image of myself on the eleven o'clock news, and it wasn't a pretty sight. I finally found the pet food aisle and grabbed a few boxes of dog cookies and made a mad dash for the checkout counter. Luckily, the "ten items or less" line was wide open. I guess I was the only person in the store who was not pushing two tons of grub in front of them. I found that Win Co shopping carts dwarf most of the other shopping carts of the world. When I got out to the parking lot, I took a deep breath. I wanted to fall to the ground and kiss it, but there was some sort of goo on the asphalt, so I passed on that idea.

When I got back to the truck, all three dogs were fast asleep. What kind of guard duty is that? They came alive when I opened the door, and all three tried to put their heads in the grocery bag at the same time that I was trying to get into the truck. I gave each one the long-awaited cookie and asked them if they knew what I had to go through to get these for them. They didn't care what I was talking about—they were too busy insisting on another cookie. I thought that this must be the way it is back in Washington DC—no one appreciates what you go through to make a couple of bucks for cookies. No appreciation at all. Just give me another cookie.

Boogie and Bentley can't wait to get to town to restock their cookie supply.

Something's Burnin', Platform Shoes, and Overcrowding

I took Tuesday with me when I went to light our burn piles across the road. As the last pile was burning down, a gust of wind came up and blew some sparks up the hill a little way, igniting a few hot spots. Up the hill I ran with a shovel and water. As I put one out, Tuesday would be running between me and the next hot spot, barking, "Here's one, you better hurry! There's one over there, too!" Although there wasn't anything to worry about (the ground was still damp), that did nothing for my runaway fire paranoia.

Years ago--many lifetimes ago—I was living in Grand Junction, Colorado, where I had a rock band called "3-Fifty-7." On a damp fall day just before band rehearsal I decided to burn some tumbleweeds out in my corrals. Anyone who has burned tumbleweeds knows they flare up as if you threw a match into a can of gasoline. As I lit my pile of tumbleweeds, a gust of wind came up and carried burning tumbleweeds into the cornfield behind my place. Drowning in sweat, my heart pounding in my throat, I watched little fires erupt all around me.

"Great, I'm going to be buying a hundred acres of popcorn."

My water hose was at least fifty feet short of reaching the cornfield, so with a shovel in hand I went into war mode. I was very glad that earlier in the day the farmer who owned the cornfield had made three or four passes with his combine, so my fire lines were at ground level rather than at the top of seven-foot corn stalks. I frantically ran from hot spot to hot spot, beating fires and shoveling dirt as I went. I had gallons of sweat running down my brow when the band showed up for rehearsal. Spilling out of the van, they ran to my rescue. Ah, rock n' roll firefighters!

It was a comedy watching four bandmates run around in six-inch platform shoes, fancy sequin shirts, hair with at least two cans of hair spray on each head, singing, "Something's burning, and I think it's corn." I wish I had a video of those so-cool rockers falling on their faces in the irrigation ditches (that's why farmers never wear platform shoes). After an eternal twenty minutes the fires were out; the band looked like they had been riding the range for a month, and I had a new paranoia about fire.

Anyway, this week, after Tuesday led me to the last little hot spot, I pulled up a seat on an old stump. Tuesday jumped up on my lap and gave me a much-needed face washing. I scanned over the land that I had opened up. The big trees (hardwoods and fir) now had pretty good spacing for the most part. I believe spacing is the key to a healthy forest.

I started thinking about people and overcrowding (or under-spacing). We have something like six billion folks on this planet now, and within twenty-five years we will have added a couple of billion more. All this crowding makes for unhealthy conditions—war, disease, famine—not to mention the question of where all the resources are going to come from. In the thirty-one years that I've lived in the

West, I've seen the overall quality of life deteriorating, and sometimes, on a bad day, I wonder if all that I've been doing with our land is for naught.

"3 fifty 7" band members Johnny Capatto and JD Rogers at the suds & Sounds in Grand Junction, Colorado, 1979

Party! That is, A Work Party

At 7:00 a.m. I was the first customer of the day at the Applegate Store. I wasn't there for biscuits and gravy, though that would have tasted good. I needed ice—ten bags to be exact (took me two trips to figure that out). I had a washtub filled with beer that had to be chilled perfectly for a work party I was having at our place.

There were fourteen friends and neighbors (folks who will do anything for a beer and a burger) coming over to help me with a thinning project up on our hillside. The plan was to work for four hours and then party the rest of the afternoon.

The sky was clear and the temperature was perfect as I directed folks up the hillside to the work area. The trees we were leaving alone were marked with yellow ribbon. Everything else got to meet a chainsaw. Man, when I saw a couple of the monster saws some of the guys had, I was a little embarrassed to pull out my itty bitty one. You know how guys are about size.

The hillside sounded like a swarm of killer bees when all the saws fired up. In no time at all there were piles of poles, firewood, and burn piles, and more than an acre of ground was opened up, so that the firs, pines and hardwoods could really grow. In another one hundred years, we'll have some old growth here at Rocky Thistle Ranch.

Every tree I cut was a "perfect ten." Yep, I got each and every one hung up in the next tree. I tried to blame my hang-ups on the fact that these trees were too crowded, which is why we were thinning in the first place, but other folks didn't have that much trouble. So I decided it was because I didn't have a *big* saw. Next time, I'm going to have the biggest one!

As folks started running out of steam, I wished I had had the forethought to hide a six-pack of beer somewhere up on the hillside. I probably could have gotten another hour of work out of these folks, but seeing as how I was the youngest one out there (by many, many years) it was just as well that I hadn't. Everyone was ready to eat.

After we came off the hillside and kicked back on our patio, I was thinking about how people talk about diversity in the woods—well, there it was, sitting all around me. Folks whose backgrounds ranged from environmentalist, governmental agencies, natural resource specialist, medicine, law, retirees, and those with no category except that they will work for beer.

Everyone had worked as a team and accomplished our goal for the day. Other than a sapling that dropped on someone answering a nature call (and he only got wet), it was a smooth day.

Folks filled their plates with burgers off the grill, spud salad, green salad, chips, cookies, soda, beer, cigars, jokes and laughs. Socializing beats the heck out of meetings.

As far as I know, Boogie, Bentley, and Tuesday were on good behavior through all of this. Nobody complained about a burger being stolen off a plate or out of a hand. I did notice, though, that all three didn't seem to be that hungry at dinnertime and there was not one burger left. Hmmm...

*The work party posing for a picture after a day of
thinning brush and trees on Roger's woodlot, 2001*

Throwing Balls, Scratching Ears, and Patting Butt

It's 6:15 a.m. and Tuesday wants to play ball. She
has dropped her ball at my feet at least a hundred times,
while I've been trying to weed and water the garden before
the sun starts to shine on our part of Thompson Creek. It's
pleasantly cool right now, but by 10 a.m. that will change.

"Okay, Tuesday, I'll take a break." This works out
well when folks want to know why I am just sitting around
in our front yard swing. I say, "I have no choice. Miss
Tuesday insists that we play ball." I lift Boogie up on the
cedar swing with me. This faithful friend's back legs are
getting really bad. She can't jump up anymore, and she'd
never pass a sobriety test as she can't walk a straight line.
She lays her head in my lap so I'll scratch her ears. She's
trained me well over the years. Now her son Bentley wants
his butt patted. I think this would be a good time to write
my editorial for the *Applegator*. The problem is I only have
two hands. So in between scratches, butt pats, and ball
throws, I write a few words at a time.

How many of you folks saw the *Time* magazine article in the July 16 [2001] issue titled "War on the West"? The Applegate got mentioned (a small paragraph) as one of the three places around the West where folks (like our Applegate Partnership and others) are trying to find solutions to natural resource issues (timber, fisheries, mining, etc.). The article stated that the Quincy Library Group in California was the first of the three to form, but that's not correct--the Applegate Partnership has that distinction. The other group mentioned was the Henry Fork Watershed Group in Ashton, Idaho. Time to throw the ball, scratch ear, and pat butt again.

Don't you think it's time for the folks in this county, this state—heck, even this country--to start working together (instead of settling for political solutions) to solve our problems with weather, social issues, natural resources, and anything else? *Time* magazine used the Applegate as an example of one of the places in the West where folks are working successfully on natural resource issues. Is there anybody out there who doesn't think we've got a mountain of problems here to overcome? And what does that say about the rest of the West? The Applegate is light years ahead of most other areas. I know. I have visited many parts of the West these past few years. I tell you, the one thing I know for certain from my travels is that if we don't get past our selfishness ("I'm right, you're wrong" or "Not in my backyard"), our tendency to make a religion of our beliefs (to cut or not cut trees, to graze or not graze cattle or sheep), our reaction to appearances (long hair or pointy-toed boots), our attitudes towards bank accounts ("We can all live in caves" or "We need every 'toy' ever invented"), we are going to go down and go down hard. We will all be wearing the big "L" on our forehead—L for Loser.

We need to manage our natural resources in a way that is best for the land, remembering that we humans are part of the equation. Some will say, "Just leave it alone, we don't need management." I say, "When European ships dropped anchor here, they didn't find a wilderness, but a land that had been managed for thousands of years (fire being one of the biggest tools) by Native Americans to try to make the land and its resources fit their needs."

There are those who want all the cream now and believe it is their right to clearcut the forest, road it, take every last drop of water from the creeks and rivers. I say life is somewhere between these two camps, and that is where we will find a sustainable management solution for our natural resources here in the Applegate.

Throwing balls, scratching ears, and patting butts—these are fun things. Problem solving for our community—that's harder, but just as rewarding.

Boogie, Bentley and Tuesday all dressed up for a party, 2001

Bye to Boogie

My bride, Sioux, and I have been very saddened by the death of our Australian Shepherd, Boogie.

For fourteen and a half years she was a great companion and constant source of amazement. It seems like only a short while ago that Sioux and I were checking out a litter of eight two-week-old puppies. Boogie wasn't the first one of the litter I held, but when it was her turn I knew she was the one. It was another four weeks before we could bring her home.

Over the years (it doesn't seem like I've been doing this paper for seven plus years), Boogie, with her adventures and shenanigans, has provided me with many stories from the editor's chair. I thought it only fitting that I reprint my favorite (although at the time I was beyond livid with her). Boogie's story appeared in the September/October 1997 issue of the *Applegator*. Oh yes, I'm sure our other two dogs, Bentley and Tuesday, will continue to provide me some good doggie tales in the future.

Boogie's poses for her first photo, 1987

Late Night Fridge Raid

I was returning home from a lovely evening spent with good friends up here on Thompson Creek. While opening the back door I was contemplating the evening's conversation and great dinner, when two of our dogs, Bentley and Tuesday, bolted by me like a flash of lightning. Oh God! That only means one thing. No, not that they needed to relieve themselves, but somebody had gotten into something.

They don't get into the trash since I fixed the cabinet door. They don't get into the bread drawer because we've moved the bread to higher ground, and there were no cookies in my broken cookie jar.

I turned the light on and couldn't believe what I was staring at. The refrigerator door was wide open, with most of the contents strung across the floor, all the way into the living room.

I just stood there, taking in the devastation. My roasted chicken was completely gone--not a morsel left. The container it had come in was as clean as a whistle. The two pounds of extra lean hamburger had been reduced to shredded pieces of Styrofoam. Sioux's box of garden burgers was empty (just as well, how can anyone eat something like that when you can get the real thing?). Two pounds of cheese—gone without a trace. A half dozen hard-boiled eggs vanished, shells and all. Two packages of flour tortillas also disappeared. The little buggers had even pulled out the milk carton. Milk mixed with water from the defrosting freezer was slowly spreading over the kitchen floor.

I should add that our refrigerator is not one of those nice side-by-side jobs, but a small apartment-size model. (The real refrigerator is in the garage because of our small kitchen.) Still, how did the dogs open the door? It had to have been Boogie, who was hiding in her corner under the stairs. She wasn't coming out for nobody or nothin'! The other two were pacing back and forth outside the back door. When I called them in, they ran to their corners in the living room without me even saying, "Go to your corner, you miserable _____!"

So I began the clean-up project at 11:00 p.m. Unbelievably, I even found teeth marks on the lid of my

Miracle Whip jar—thank God they didn't get into that. The plastic shelf from the refrigerator had been pulled out and broken. I was starting to think these dogs had become a pack of juvenile delinquents. I went to get the mop, only to find that the sponge, which was poorly glued on it, was gone.

Oh, right, I was supposed to get a replacement for it. I checked, and it's still on my list. Well, this was just great. I had to get down on my hands and knees with paper towels to sop up the mess. The three villains in this story kept looking around the corner at me, and I kept sending them back to their corners, telling them they might be there forever and then some. I wound up mopping (by hand) the kitchen and dining area and finally crawled off to bed around 1:00 a.m. Literally crawled, because now my back was aching from mopping the floors.

After a very poor night's sleep, during which the dogs finally snuck into the bedroom and into their own beds, the love of my life (my wife, Sioux) called from San Francisco to wish me a happy birthday (I know, thirty-six, *HA!*). I told her, in colorful but restrained detail, all the previous evening's events. Between her giggles and snickers, she said, "You know, honey, now you have your next *Applegator* story!"

Good Thing or Bad Thing?

I've been pondering this question for a long time. Is management of our national monuments and parks a good thing or a bad thing? Of course, that all depends on your definition of a good thing or a bad thing. So, with a little history, I'll give you some definitions.

When I was a twelve-year-old boy with the misfortune of living in a miserable, humid, overcrowded, God-fearing, cockroach-infested place called Indiana, I got to go west to Utah for the first time with old friends of our family, Fred Radcliff (who had been going to Utah since the uranium boom of the 1950s) and his twelve-year-old son Bernie. It was during a spring vacation--a vacation I prayed would never end. That adventure to Arches National Monument (now a national park) in southeastern Utah was my undoing. I'd never seen anything (except for a few women) so beautiful. It was love at first sight.

I was drawn to the Red Rock Canyon country like a gray squirrel to traffic or a moth to a bug light. I just couldn't help myself. The sheer rock walls rose 300, 500, 700 feet straight up to the bluest of blue Utah skies; misshapen, gnarly juniper trees grew out of cracks in solid sandstone (how did they do that?); pinon trees, rabbit brush, sage brush, prickly pear cactus, barrel cactus with flowers in shades from lavender to red amazed me. I never saw another soul while we were there. By God, this was real wilderness, and for a kid from Indiana entering the nightmare of adolescence, this was a good place to be.

Fred would idle his old International Travelall up and over the slick rock roads, race down the washes through quicksand and out again before we were mired up to the frame. We rattled down the most rutted, miserable washboard excuse of a trail I had ever been on, and this was a good thing!

Now more than a million tourists zoom through the arches at sixty miles an hour on a paved road wide enough for a triple trailer rig. No more quicksand to drive through. Bridges now span those washes—there were too many tourists perishing (but in my mind not nearly enough). Asphalt parking areas complete with stripes (don't want any confusion), where one can view the arches from the comforts of an air-conditioned car or motorhome, never having to leave the sardine can. These are bad things!

Fred, Bernie, and I would throw our sleeping bags on the ground, gather a little firewood, cook up an elegant gourmet meal of hot dogs on a stick with roasted marshmallows, and chase it all down with a Dr. Pepper. Man, we were living! If you had to answer nature's call, you'd just find the nearest cedar tree—not too difficult. As we finished reminiscing about the adventures of the day and discussing the glories we'd find tomorrow, I'd notice the silence of the night. I'd never heard this kind of quiet before. As I lay there in my army surplus sleeping bag with the broken zipper, I became hypnotized by the sound of my beating heart while the full moon rose over the mighty snow-capped peaks of the La Sal Mountains to the south. When the last embers of our fire flickered and died, I heard my first coyote yipping in the far distance, followed by an owl hooting from a nearby pinon tree. Yes, if there is such a place as heaven, I had found it. This was a good thing!

Now, if you're not an outlaw, you have to camp in designated posted areas with asphalt under your rig, picnic tables, trash cans, neighbors close enough to spit watermelon seeds at, modern restrooms, drinking water, the hum of generators spewing their stench so that these aluminum beer cans on wheels can have electricity for lights, motors to pump water to their sinks, toilets, and showers, security lighting, and power for the satellite dish so the whole camp can be forced to listen to the latest in bad canned laughter from the newest and dumber-than-dumb sitcom. Yes, the evil deeds of industrialized tourism. This is a bad thing!

Back then there weren't signs everywhere we went, and there was only one ranger, whom we never saw. We hiked out to Delicate Arch, one of the greatest sculpted formations in the West, on a trail that wasn't much to begin with and definitely wasn't much maintained. It ran across a lot of slick rock with potholes still filled with spring rainwater, teeming with all sorts of creatures I'd never seen before. If you really, really tried you might get lost, and maybe, just maybe, you'd fall prey to a mountain lion that had grown fat and lazy from feeding on tasty mule deer. Or you might come down with Rocky Mountain tick fever, or fall by the wayside overcome by gnats, deer flies, blow flies, or scorpions. Then you might feel lucky to find a water hole, only to learn later it was arsenic water. But probably you would just succumb to plain old common everyday heat stroke—even in April. All this was a good thing!

Now there are signs everywhere: "Restrooms, 1 mi. ahead," " Don't pet or feed the scorpions, tarantulas, or rattlesnakes," "Don't drink the water," "Carry water at all times," "No collecting of rocks, firewood, or arrowheads," "No hunting," "Keep pets on a leash." There are dozens and dozens of employees and rangers to provide the answers to all of the tourists' questions that the signs already tell them.

The trails are all well-groomed parkways. Some have even been paved, and still some foreigners get lost. Mountain lions have definitely not acquired a taste for tourists. I guess they are just too high in fat and cholesterol. Now the tourists have multiplied beyond the carrying capacity of the land. This is a bad thing!

All this used to be free, if you didn't count all the taxes we pay ordinarily. Now there are admission fees, trail fees, river fees, camping fees, and special stamp fees. It's no wonder this Disneyland doesn't come cheap with all its paved roads, Holiday Inn camping areas, 3,000-foot-deep water wells. There's also search and rescue for those who don't read the forest of signs, as well as the salaries, medical insurance, dental insurance, vision insurance, unemployment insurance, retirement plans, uniforms, badges, ticket books, mace, guns, bullets, training maneuvers, helicopters, airplanes, toilet paper, Band-Aids, light bulbs, social workers, and mental health specialists. Yes, Arches is part of the twenty-first century. This is a bad thing!

But there are those outlaws who know the back ways into the Arches and its farthest corners, that only the Anasazi Indians and wayward cows knew about. So under the cover of darkness, on a moonless night, my bride Sioux and I can hike in with Bentley and Tuesday (without leashes) and recover that long-forgotten hole-in-the-rock-gang experience. This is a good thing!

Phone Rage

Why aren't there real people working the phone lines when you have the misfortune to have to call some company about a problem you're having, be it billing or warranty or some information you need?

Good Lord, there's no shortage of folks needing work—unemployment is six percent or more. We all know that figure is way low. The feds have this magic formula that keeps these numbers down: people discharged from the military; people not collecting unemployment, people not registered at the Employment Office, and so forth, don't count. There are plenty of folks trained in phone work, as America now has the distinction of having more workers in phone solicitation than in factory work. Scary! Phone solicitation has one of the highest employment turnover rates, as well as offering no benefits and "great pay"—minimum wage. What did factory workers used to make?

Anyway, I want to know if it bugs you as much as me when I'm calling, let's say, Torture and Torture Incorporated, and I get a recording saying "Hello. You've reached the offices of Torture and Torture. Your call may be recorded for quality control and training purposes, for your convenience." (When I hear the words "For your convenience," I automatically bend over and grab my ankles, because I know it's a lie and someone wants into my wallet.) Anyway, then I'm told to please follow the menu.

"For Spanish, push one; for Somalian, push two; for Rastafarian, push three; for Ebonics, push four," etc., until finally, "For English, push nine, or if you know the extension of the person with whom you wish to speak, enter that number now." Who are they kidding? I wish I knew Putz Baloney's extension number, but that is top secret information. Or "If you know the name of the person with whom you wish to speak, push star and say their name." Okay, so I say, "Putz Baloney."

"If Frank Malloy is whom you wish to speak to, push the pound button. If not, push star and repeat name." So I repeat Putz Baloney's name.

"If Bob Shupe is whom you wish to speak to, push the pound button." I'm going nuts. Maybe I'm speaking with an Indianan/Utahan accent that the mechanical voice doesn't understand.

By this point I want to start banging my phone on the kitchen table, but these new phones aren't made like a good old 1956 model. One or two hits with the new portable phones and you are out a hundred bucks, but with an old 1956 or earlier you can turn your kitchen table into kindling—or scrap iron if it's a metal table.

I think the folks who develop these phone menus are sadists who must have worn wet black leather skullcaps at one time. After the cap dried and shrunk, there was so much pressure put on that tiny grain of sand called a brain that they came up with the mental terrorist act now known as a "phone menu."

I push nine for English and the mechanical menu voice says, "Push one for 'Do you have a future'?" Oh, that could be frightening.

"Push two for your current debt load. Push three for death benefits. Push four to repeat these options, or stay on the line for the next available representative."

I hope they are recording my call, as I scream into the phone, "You stupid, fatheaded, dimwit! I hate your mechanical voice! I'm praying that Torture and Torture Inc. goes the same route as Enron!" I want Torture and Torture Inc. to have to pay for any phone menu agony I'm suffering. I understand that because of corporations such as these there are many groups now calling for retroactive abortion legislation.

After five more minutes, I'm still waiting for the next available representative to come on the line. I'm forced to listen to some god-awful music that sounds like fingernails on a chalkboard. Every minute or two that nauseating voice comes on the line and thanks me for my patience. I wonder how many people went through one of these phone menus before they snapped and wound up on the eleven o'clock news for committing some heinous crime. Is phone rage a legal defense these days?

Right now every muscle in my body is wound so tight I feel I could explode. I have sweat on my brow, and I feel a migraine coming on. I start pacing through the house, utilizing the one advantage of having a cordless phone. That's when I discover that one of our dogs, Bentley or Tuesday (or maybe both of them), has pulled a full roll of toilet paper from the bathroom rack, and it is now strung down the hallway and all over our bedroom. I call both dogs and have started to read the riot act to them when there is a click on the phone, and I hear "Welcome to Torture and Torture, Inc. Push one for Spanish."

The Coast Range Is Gone? or Doo Doo the Wonder Dog

This past week I made a trip up to Portland Airport to pick up my parents, who flew in from Texas to visit for a week. My mother has wanted to see the whole Oregon coast, so I planned a two-day trip starting in Astoria, which I think was the nicest town of the whole trip.

The Oregon coast is so beautiful—in fact, "beautiful" is an understatement—as long as you don't look inland to the coast range forest. Actually, I don't believe there is a coast range forest any more. There are a few pockets of "what once was" in the form of state parks and such. The coast range along Highway 101 has been reduced to miles and miles of stumps or that new type of old growth forest where trees tower at staggering heights of twenty-five to thirty feet with gigantic girths of two to fifteen inches. How could a forest that once had such grandeur be reduced to trees fit only for gnomes?

Thinning doesn't seem to be in the vocabulary of coast range forest management, where I found awesome twigs of thirty feet in height in such dense thickets one could not even crawl through them. Why wasn't there long-term management planning for these forests, like we're trying to do in the Applegate? I know that if planning had been done for the long haul investment (where we would always have a mix of old growth trees) instead of the next fiscal quarter, maybe we wouldn't have all these timber wars.

Long before our dogs Tuesday, Bentley, and the late, great Boogie, I had an Australian mix dog named DooDoo. (That's the French pronunciation.) He earned his name for failing Potty Training 101 for over a year.

Back in those days, I rode with the infamous Holiday Gang out of Moab, Utah. We were tagged with this name by Police Chief Mel Dalton because we all lived and worked at the Holiday Theater. The building was on its last legs (it's now a parking lot). The doors were warped; the roof had many leaks, and the wiring was museum quality. We had refurbished the old coal bin with two chairs from the dump, a wood cable spool for a table, and four old mattresses on the floor for sleeping. The mattresses also made for a softer landing when you entered our digs by way of the coal chute in the back alley.

I was one of three highly trained professional projectionists. In this legally-approved profession I earned a gigantic salary of seven to ten dollars a day. That's all I needed back then. I loved my two-day work week. All of our spare time was spent fishing, hunting, riding, or hiking the La Sal Mountains, or exploring the awesome red rock canyon lands.

DooDoo was well known around Moab. He had many food stops, such as the eye doctor's office, post office, Frank's Tavern, etc. He was the dog about town. When I would be running a movie, DooDoo would be kept down in the "Bin," as we referred to our coal-bin pad. There was a door from the basement to the stage in front of the movie screen.

One evening while I was running a John Wayne Western, in the middle of a great shoot-out DooDoo appeared on the stage (somebody forgot to close the door tight). A kid in the front row started calling to DooDoo, who began to bark as he ran in circles chasing his tail. He then stood at the edge of the stage, looking out over the audience and emitting barks that seemed to say, "Look at me, I'm a star." All this while John Wayne was finishing off the bad guys.

The ushers that night--Ken Hoffman and Phillip Hurtado—were at each end of the stage on the stairs, trying to call DooDoo to them. Of course, he thought they wanted to play, so he ran down the stairs between Phillip's legs, knocking him off the stairs and onto the kids sitting in the front row. Up the aisle DooDoo ran barking, and out into the lobby, making an old man drop his popcorn and soda (I had to pay for that), and then back down the other aisle, scooting between Ken's legs and back up on the stage.

By this time, Andy Contreras, the lady who owned the theater, was hollering at me on the intercom to come get my DooDoo (I thought that sounded funny). I left the projection booth, ran across the theater roof, slid down the ladder in the storeroom, stormed across the lobby and into the theater that was by that time a mass of confusion.

DooDoo came to me as soon as I called him. I picked him up and climbed the stairs to the stage while the Duke was taking aim. Then the unthinkable happened—the film ran out. The screen turned white as the movie house was lit up. With DooDoo under my arm, I stood on stage as a thundering round of applause, hoots, and hollers filled the theater. It seems that DooDoo's performance was more popular than Duke's. Thank you, DooDoo!

JD and Doo Doo the Wonder Dog on a fall camping trip to the La Sal Mountaians, Utah, 1974

Campaigns and Dogs

The Civil War—man, I'm glad I missed that one.

Frederick H. Dyer tabulated that there were 10,455 military "events" during the Civil War. From 1861 to 1865 fighting took place on approximately 1,396 days, with an estimated 623,000 soldiers killed. It's amazing we ever recovered from such bloodletting!

One thing I find fascinating about the Civil War is the great number of mascots that traveled with so many of the regiments. Wisconsin had three regiments that took badgers to war with them. A confederate unit from Arkansas traveled with a wildcat. Then there was the Louisiana regiment that took a pelican to battle, according to the book *Civil War Curiosities* by Webb Gassison. There's an account of a barnyard hen that became so attached to General Lee during his invasion of Pennsylvania that she followed him for weeks, nesting under his cot each night.

The menagerie of mascots covered everything from bears, lambs, squirrels, pigeons, camels, and crows, to a bald eagle named "Old Abe" who went into battle with the Eighth Wisconsin Regiment. At the sound of a regimental bugle, that Old Abe had learned to recognize, he'd take flight and soar high above the battlefield out of musket range. From the winter of 1862 to the end of the Civil War, Old Abe flew over campaigns in New Madrid, Fort Pillow, Hamburg Landing, Vicksburg and many others. He was so well known to the Confederates that they referred to him as that "Yankee Buzzard." After the war Old Abe took up residence in the capitol at Madison, Wisconsin, where he lived until 1904, when he died of smoke inhalation after the capitol burned.

Of course, my favorite mascot stories are about dogs (the most popular mascot), and the campaigns they survived during the Civil War. There was Captain Werner Von Bachelle from an Ohio brigade who had trained his dog to perform all kinds of feats, including military salutes. The two were inseparable. In fact, after the Union abandoned its frontline at the Battle of Antietam, Captain Bachelle's body was found later with his dog standing guard. The Fourth Louisiana Brigade had a bird dog named Sawbuck who roamed at will and knew nearly every member of the division. When the bugle sounded for an assault, Sawbuck always went into battle running up and down the line barking his encouragement to the men.

In the days that I campaigned across the Southwest (although not in a war) with the "Utah Outlaws," we left a lot of "scorched earth" of a different type. Our mascot at that time was DooDoo the Wonder Dog. Wherever we made camp old DooDoo would spend hours staring up into a tree trying to figure out a way to catch one of the squirrels that always chattered at him. I assumed he found it maddening not being able to climb a tree to catch one of his tormentors, for he moved from tree to tree making a high-pitched whimper as he followed the squirrel.

On one particular campaign, the notorious Utah Outlaw Chris "Madman" Allen and I stopped for the view from the Grand Canyon's North Rim. I'm sure it would have been a magnificent sight, except that the South Rim was lost in a haze of smoke spewing forth from the Four Corners Power Plant so Southern Californians could have air conditioning.

Chris and I had just finished a pre-lunch treat and were being amused by the chipmunks that abounded around the parking lot. These chipmunks were as large as guinea pigs, and no wonder: Hordes of tourists were feeding them peanuts, bread crumbs, or whatever else was at hand. These cute, obese rodents would waddle from handout to handout, while posing for an array of Japanese cameras clicking away. I overheard one tourist, who looked a lot like the chipmunk he was feeding, say, "By golly Ma, isn't this wildlife and nature swell?" You bet buddy, I thought, nature paved in asphalt and enveloped in smog.

I had just made myself a Miracle Whip sandwich while seated on the tailgate of Chris's pick-up when I was stopped in mid-bite by a blood-curdling, ear-piercing scream. My God, I thought, someone must have cartwheeled over the rim. I dropped my Miracle Whip sandwich reluctantly and grabbed my camera. As I turned to run toward the scream that was still penetrating every crevice of the park, I thought, "It's a long way to the bottom." No, that wasn't it. DooDoo the Wonder Dog was proudly prancing towards me with a poster-child-for-weight-watchers chipmunk in his mouth, that he then dropped at our feet.

A boy of seven or eight had been feeding this particular chipmunk when DooDoo snagged it, his one and only chipmunk ever. The boy's mother was comforting her obviously traumatized-for-life son, who I'm sure had many years ahead of him on some shrink's couch. A large crowd of male tourists in flip-flops, plaid Bermuda shorts, and xxx-large Hawaiian shirts started to gather around while their wives, with white pasty uncooked jelly-roll complexions, looked on aghast. One guy hollered, "That there your dog?" DooDoo's tail was wagging 100 miles per hour as he sat proudly in front of me. I responded, "Nice shoes you're wearing." His response was, "Huh?" as he looked down toward his flip-flops, which he couldn't see over the enormous gut he had acquired from all the cases of beer he had consumed over the years. Another guy piped up, "Hey buddy, you got a license for that dog?" As the boy's whimper died down, the crowd seemed to be growing more hostile. I said, "Yes, sir, this dog is licensed to catch chipmunks." By this time Chris had loaded DooDoo and our lunches into the truck and had fired up the engine. From somewhere in the back of the crowd someone hollered, "I never heard of no such thing!" As I got in the pick-up, I mentioned that we were from Utah. That seemed to bring a momentary calm to the mob, as they just looked at each other with blinking eyes.

Chris was driving the wrong way out of the parking lot when we passed a Park Rangerette moving at a fast trot with her hand resting on her mace can.

I guess the gist of all of this is that scratching a dog's ears is relaxing. However, a dog with a chipmunk in its mouth could be stressful, what with bail money, attorney's fees, paperwork, and chain gang work. Today you would add Homeland Security, involving 100 different federal agencies, and smallpox and anthrax vaccine for all involved.

But being from Utah had its advantages--we knew all the back roads.

Survivor

Survivor. That's a word I know quite a bit about—head-on car crashes, rollovers, careening over sixty-foot drop-offs, uranium ore train crashes at 1,600 feet underground, and even the world of rock-and-roll. Then there's having a ruptured appendix for over a day and, not long ago, another surgery where my stomach was visiting my heart. My feet have been held to the fire on several other occasions, too.

My worst experience happened over thirty-nine years ago in Indianapolis. I still remember it vividly. A few weeks ago a memorial was held honoring this tragedy. On October 31, 1963, my grandparents, Paul and Marietta Mason, took my two sisters, Paula and Kandy, my brother Jeff, and me to see "The Holiday on Ice Review" in the coliseum at the Indiana State Fairgrounds. My mother was in the hospital being prepared for surgery, so she and my father had given their tickets to my grandparents' best friends, Jess and Roxie Curtis.

At 11:04 p.m., as the grand finale was starting, two explosions ripped through a section of box seats just up a few rows from where we were all seated.

As I was picking myself up from among the massive debris of concrete, chairs, and bodies, flames were licking at the ceiling of the coliseum from a huge hole where two faulty propane tanks had leaked gas into a sealed room and then blown up. I was a twelve-year-old boy in the middle of this nightmare telling myself to wake up. I realized this was no dream, when I saw my grandpa, who was dead, and my grandma, who was covered with rubble and begging me to help her. My brother had reached out and grabbed my ankle through two huge slabs of concrete that had pinned him to the floor. I tried to pull him out from under the concrete, but couldn't budge him.

My world was reeling in this hellscape of smoke, fire, and groans and screams of death as I started to feel the chunks of concrete imbedded in my own back and head. As I drifted in and out of shock, I was loaded into a paddy wagon (the only time I've ever been in a paddy wagon) and taken to an emergency room that looked like a MASH unit with wounded and dying everywhere.

I must have looked worse than I was, because I was listed in the newspaper the next day as dead. My two sisters, my brother, and I survived, but all who sat immediately around us perished. Seventy-four people died altogether, my grandparents and the Curtises among them. Hundreds were injured.

About a year and a half ago my mother, Shirley Rogers, spearheaded a movement to have a plaque erected at the coliseum in memory of those who died that night. With the help of our cousin, Richard Basore, the media, and the Indiana State Fair Board, my mother's dream was realized.

Many people have survived the pains of war, tragedy and heartbreak. Some lock these events far away in their minds. Others plummet to the bottom of life's ladder, and yet others find religion or reasoning for such events. I believe the one thread that holds true for all traumatic experiences is that you never forget.

Survivor! Even my dogs have experienced such things. DooDoo the Wonder Dog had many close shaves with death.

My first trip to the West Coast (from Moab, Utah) was with Utah's notorious outlaw Chris "Madman" Allen and DooDoo. We had just left San Francisco where we stood out like sore thumbs (not many Mountain-Man-looking folks in San Francisco). We had driven across the Golden Gate Bridge in Chris's gold '76 Datsun pick-up at the break-neck speed of fifteen miles per hour (tourists!). Traffic raced by with many motorists waving their index finger at us, but we were lost in deep conversation about the Golden Gate Bridge.

"Oooh, check that out, dude."

"Heavy."

"What's smokin'?" Etcetera.

We parked on the Marin side of the bridge and walked back to the center to watch an aircraft carrier sail into the bay. I was in a deep-transit state of thought (I know that's hard to believe), when squealing car brakes and the smell of burning rubber brought me back to reality. My God, I thought, I'm going to witness a great pile-up on the Golden Gate Bridge. I couldn't believe my eyes as I turned toward the traffic, and there stood DooDoo the Wonder Dog. He had jumped through the window screen on the camper and was now in the middle of the Golden Gate Bridge, eating chicken bones from a Kentucky Fried Chicken thrift box someone had tossed out.

With all traffic stopped, I darted out across the lanes of traffic to rescue DooDoo from his natural selection fate and possibly my own. A construction worker from the bridge paint crew made sure traffic stayed stopped in the inbound lanes. Who knows how far back in either direction the traffic had been disrupted by this chicken-bone crunching dog and his buckskin-clad sidekick. Chris had the right idea about then:

"Wow man, we better head to the redwoods and lie low for a while."

With horns honking, fists shaking, and obscenities flying our way from angry motorists, Chris's idea sounded "primo" to me.

Survivor! We've all survived something at one time or another in our lives. Have you ever wondered why?

JD rescuing Doo Doo the wonder Dog from his adventure out on the Golden Gate Bridge. Chris "Mad Man" Allen took the picture figuring it would be the last time he would see me or Doo Doo since he figured natural selection was about to take its course, 1974.

Deep Doo-Doo

I was laughing until my sides hurt this morning. I had been listening to my favorite radio show out of Indianapolis, "The Bob and Tom Show." They were talking about some lady who hadn't been watching where she was walking while visiting her local PetSmart store. She slipped in some dog doo-doo in one of the aisles and fell to the floor with a splat. Now she's suing PetSmart.

People sue for a lot of stupid things: falling off a ladder, hot coffee spilled in laps, etc., but dog doo-doo in the aisle of a pet store? Come on! The settlement of this lawsuit (the pain and suffering part) will add a new category to our legal system known hence- forth as Doo-Doo Damages. After such a traumatic experience, can you imagine the nightmares you might endure? Like "Night of the Living Dog Doo-Doo." Dude, that's scary to think about.

I'm sure that in the future PetSmart stores will have to hire people to patrol the aisles armed with, you got it, Doggie Doo Scoopers. I wonder how you'd word that job description on your resume? What kind of retirement party would you have after twenty years on the Doggie Doo Scooper Patrol? Would you get the Golden Scoop? Of course, this will be a unionized job, called Doggie Doo Scooper Patrol of America or simply Local D.D.S.P. Workers will have to serve a five-year apprenticeship before being allowed to walk the aisles alone with an armed and loaded scooper.

The country will grind to a halt when the local D.D.S.P. goes out on strike for such things as rubber gloves made-to-last, respirators with better air filters, or no robotics to be used for Doggie Doo Scooper Patrols. Just think about the interesting worker's compensation cases there will be, such as "I have no idea how this Doo Scooper became embedded in my, let's see, oh, yes, my forehead" or "Hey Dude, if you had followed Great Danes around for ten years, your back would have gone out, too." The repercussions from these suits will shake the very foundation of this country.

Now that I think about it, Sioux and I are very lucky our good friend Rick Costanza (some of you may remember him from the great punk band Ricky Lee Costanza and the Plutoniums) didn't sue us a while back when he paid us a visit. It was a dark, hot summer night, so Rick decided to throw his sleeping bag on our front lawn. That's right, you guessed it. Come morning, Rick awoke not to the smell of the great outdoors, but rather to the smell of doggie doo-doo because he had thrown his sleeping bag in the doggie doo-doo corner of our yard. I had seen that right off, but said nothing. Hey, what's a buddy for?

Back to PetSmart. Bentley and Tuesday have never been to one. I guess I'll take them soon. I'll let them wander the aisles, checking out the latest in food bowls with assorted accessories, rawhide chew bones, artificial-flavored dog cookies, aerodynamic and hip-looking throwing balls for Tuesday, and large, cushy, comfy sleeping beds for Bentley. I'll be checking out the Doggie

Doo-Doo scoopers, in case Rick ever comes back for a visit.

Actually, I'm sure when this lawsuit is settled, any dog even found in the parking lot of a PetSmart will be in deep doo-doo.

European Wedding and Biological Bugs

Sioux and I recently spent two weeks in Europe. That was a first for me. Although I lived in a foreign land called Utah for sixteen years, Europe was quite different.

We spent a week in beautiful Prague in the Czech Republic. We took lodging off the beaten path and away from the tourist areas. Prague is filled with many magical architectural gems. I was surprised there were any places that had not been overrun by tourists--or locusts, as I refer to them. (I know, I had become a locust myself.)

This historical city hasn't been swallowed up by that American cancer known as "box stores." That's right—no super Wal-Marts, and we saw very few fast food choke-and-puke restaurants. One can actually sample some culture at the hundreds of local shops, restaurants, and markets. The markets, which were my favorite, had fruits and vegetables, and there were bakeries where we could buy freshly-made pastries and bread. (Not like that white fluff that you get in the U.S. It's a "Wonder" that we call it bread.)

The Czech Republic has a mass transit system that even someone with my diminished brain capacity (too many years playing a game called "rock butting," where I didn't know you were supposed to wear a helmet) could quickly figure out. Okay, okay—my private nurse and wife Sioux figured it out, but I did lead the way down all the little alleys we explored (I've got longer legs).

Next we headed to Slovakia for the royal wedding of Weston Taussig (Sioux's son) and Monika Suranska. The wedding was held at the Bojnice Castle, which was more magnificent than any fairy tale you've ever read. Monika was the most beautiful bride I've ever seen—except for my wife Sioux. The reception/party lasted two days. I was amazed that at two a.m. there were aunts and grannies all the way up into their late eighties who were getting down to techno music. I think I experienced my first rave.

I did manage to compete a little with the techno tunes, as my song "Spirit of the Rose" was played, and, by golly, it was requested again, so that it played back to back. That made me feel really good.

Sioux was running hard with the male Slovakians as they traded shots of Black Death Tequila with live worms in each shot glass. Me, I checked out the buffet of roasted pigs, vegetables, fruits, and some of the best pastry I've ever eaten. What a treat! No worms for me!

We headed back to Prague, to find the highway was closed due to a wreck. I'm surprised there aren't many more. Anyone who has been to Europe knows speed limits (what's that?) and no passing zones are for someone else. By the time we got to the station in Prague, the train was pulling out. We had our suitcases handed up through the train window as we left the station heading for Frankfurt. Unlike here, when a train is scheduled to leave at 3:13 p.m., it leaves at 3:13 p.m., not 8:05 p.m.

Then it hit. No, not a meteor or a rocket, but what Sioux and I first thought was food poisoning. A sleeper compartment with six people is not where you want to be under those conditions. We basically moved our compartment to the commode section of the train. At 2:30 a.m., while we were lying in a delirious state, the door to our sleeping compartment was flung open, and a heavily accented male voice hollered, "Passports!" Staring into a flashlight with my eyes rolled to the back of my head, soaked in perspiration, I handed the guard our passports and started thinking of that old movie *Midnight Express*. I figured I fit a profile and could be placed in an institution where my worst nightmare could become reality. After what seemed like an eternity, the guard finally left us to our misery.

Feeling weak and dizzy when we got off the train in Frankfurt, we boarded our next train to Amsterdam. Sioux said, "Honey, I don't think this is the right train." Of course, being male, I told her not to worry; I'm an old Mountain Man, and I had guided us to the right train. You guessed it; it was the wrong train. Being sick came in handy as I drowned in my sea of excuses. Always listen to your nurse, I should know that. Luckily, half a dozen stops later we were able to catch the correct train.

We sure wanted to see Amsterdam, but we mostly saw it from the window of the bed and breakfast where we stayed. After several days we knew our sickness wasn't food poisoning, but rather some unknown, biological Houdini bug.

The flight to San Francisco was utter misery. Of course, airlines, like concerts, never have enough restrooms, especially when you have two folks in our condition.

Once we got to San Francisco, we stayed at Sioux's brother Ira's house. Feeling better the next day, Sioux headed home to relieve our house sitter. As for me, I hung out for four days in our nephew Jeremy's room before I was finally able to make the drive home. I wondered how Jeremy would feel when he came home to find that Uncle JD had had a hospital stay in his room. I'm sure my brother-in-law had to burn everything in Jeremy's room and seal that part of the house off for the next hundred years. God only knows what destructive biological parasites I was carrying.

Many folks who attended the wedding reception got sick, and a few even went to the hospital, but this dreaded bug lasted only a few days for most of them. But not me. I'm special. After many medical tests, with no conclusions, I suffered through a long thirty-day recovery period. Finally, I'm back to normal, whatever that is. The up side is that this unidentified biological diet plan took me from 212 to 189 pounds in just days. Yeh!

I do look forward to a return trip, minus whatever super-bug it was that we caught.

Sioux on the Charles Bridge in Prague after son Weston's wedding to Monica, 2003

Wall Street Predators and Dog Cookies

This cold, frosty, blue-sky morning finds me in "downtown" Applegate at Eve's Garden Café—definitely my favorite hangout. The women there treat me as if it were 1955. The pillows are all fluffed up for me on the bench seat at the table where I usually sit. My coffee is waiting--hot, with just the exact amount of cream I like. They do all of this with a smile that shows their desire to please the customer. Yes, they do make me feel comfortable and appreciated.

In between bites of my scrumptious breakfast burrito, I take part in the conversation at my table. The participants are solving the world's problems, ranging from the war in Iraq, deficit spending, unemployment, bullying at the local schools, and the ever-present taxes. One thing almost everyone agrees on is the problem of the financial terrorists that have been allowed to run rampant on Wall Street. It started big time with Enron, Arthur Anderson, and World Com a few years ago, and to date, there haven't been any real consequences for the leaders of these anti-American institutions. The guy who knocks off a 7-Eleven would already be doing hard time for five, ten, or twenty years, but not the fat cat (with a soft underbelly) Wall Street predators.

Fortunately, the problems Sioux and I have been dealing with on the home front lately are not as large in magnitude as the above. We've been without a kitchen for seven weeks. We had to replace the floor in our dining room and kitchen. There have been delays, setbacks, and excuses one after another since the project was started.

Sioux has weathered this inconvenience rather well. She definitely has pioneer stock. Instead of eating out every night or ordering Chinese take-out (it's a long drive to town) she's adapted to cooking at night on a one-burner butane stove. With a flashlight in one hand, a kitchen utensil in the other, and all bundled up against the cold, she cooks up killer meal after killer meal. She says it's like camping out except that at night we get to crawl into our own comfy bed.

When Sioux heads back down to San Francisco to work at the V.A. Hospital, I go into my bachelor-eating mode. I revert to the days when I lived in the coal bin with no kitchen at the Holiday Theater in Moab, Utah. All I needed was a can opener and a spoon. What could be easier? The clean-up process was especially easy. I'd open a cold can of ravioli, clam chowder, or Bake-N-Beans and dig in.

Bentley and Tuesday aren't exactly joyful about my bachelor diet. They're used to getting fancy sauces or good leftovers added to their dry dog food, which makes that bland-looking stuff much more enticing. They've trained us well. When I share a cold ravioli with them I can see the question in their eyes, "Where is mama?" I know they feel they're being abused with some sort of food-like substance that is not identifiable. This tends to give me a guilt complex, so I give them extra dog cookies. I have to be careful that I don't overdo it. I don't want them to plump up to the point where I'd have to take them to doggie workout classes.

The other night when I was hungry, I was eyeing one of these dog cookies that come in every color of the rainbow. I wondered whether they had a good flavor. Sioux once told me that when her son, Weston, was a teething toddler, she'd give him dog cookies to gum on, and he seemed to enjoy them. I've noticed since Weston is all grown up now he doesn't run around marking trees any more than the next guy, so I guess his dog cookie experience hasn't left any visible negative residuals.

With a dog cookie in hand, an old memory came racing back to me. Years ago my good Utah outlaw buddy J. Michael Pearce (formerly of the J. Michael Pearce Band) stopped by on a sweltering hot day. Naturally, I offered him a cold beer, which Mike thought was a great idea at any time. Being the prankster I am, I gave him what looked like a cold bottle of beer, but was really something called "Doggie Brew"—a tasty gravy for your dog's next meal. Mike took a big swig of Doggie Brew, and I thought he was going to die. He ran to the sink, which he had trouble finding because his eyes were rolled to the back of his head, where he proceeded to gag and spit until he could rinse out his mouth. I asked, "Is your beer flat?" with a laugh. Referring to me as different body parts, he said that was the most disgusting thing he had ever tasted. Well, I've known Mike for thirty-five years, and I know he's eaten some really disgusting things, so it must have been really bad.

With this memory foremost in my ever-slowing mind, I decided not to take a chance on sampling the dog cookie. Could it be payback time for the Doggie Brew escapade? Why take a chance?

But the ones who do need a payback are the rabid, predator terrorists on Wall Street who have stolen the bank. The sooner the better.

Dogs, Recycling, and Pizza

Several weeks ago a friend and I decided we'd have ourselves a "bachelor night" of videos and pizza. The intelligent ones from each of our households (the ladies) were out of town. I volunteered to pick up the pizza, as I was going to be in town running errands anyway.

I loaded Tuesday and Utah into the truck cab, along with the many empty chicken-feed bags that were now overflowing with cans and bottles marked for recycling. Tuesday took her place in the passenger seat, while Utah stretched out on the back seat among the feedbags.

When I arrived at the store, there was the usual long line in front of the recycling machine, so I decided to run other errands first. I stopped at Papa Murphy's Pizza and picked up an Italian pizza ready to cook. Then I looped back to the recycling machine. There was now a light rain falling, and not a soul to be found at the recycle center.

Parking my truck next to the machine, I hopped out and offloaded my returns into a shopping cart. From there, I dumped a load into the aluminum can machine, so it could do its slow job of counting, leaving me free to feed bottles, one at a time, into the bottle machine. I find it insufferably maddening how slowly these modern machines of the high-tech world work.

After six bottles the machine jammed, and the can machine showed that it had rejected at least one-third of my returns. I walked over to the conveniently-placed call box (obviously this is an ongoing problem). I pushed the little red button (too bad it doesn't detonate these torturous machines from the Dark Side) and waited. No response, so I pushed the button again and waited some more--still nothing—so once again I pushed the button. After what seemed like an eternity in purgatory, a voice squawked at me, "Can I help you?" I thought, but didn't say, "Why else would anyone be calling you on this call box? To see how your grandmother is doing? To see if you're registered to vote? Or maybe it's Ed McMahon to say that you're the winner of the multimillion dollar give-away."

Instead of expressing any of those thoughts, I replied, "Hello, the bottle machine is jammed." The voice on the little box came back at me with, "Can I help you?" Great, a communication failure. I wondered if the person I was trying to talk to was in India, what with all the outsourcing going on. Not to worry. On the third try we communicated, and the clerk said, "I'll be right out." It developed that the phrase "right out" had a totally different meaning to him than it did to me.

When the clerk finally appeared, he quickly unjammed the machine. I asked him if we could just count up my returns, as the can machine was rejecting so many. The clerk informed me that I had to use the machine and asked me if I had read the sign above it. Only 144 returns per person, per day, and only returns from products sold at this store are accepted. I pointed out that most of my rejected cans were Pepsi, and that this store had sold them to me. As the clerk walked back into the store, he said to me over his shoulder, "Try running your rejects through the machine again." At that particular moment a hard rain and a cold wind cut loose.

I continued to check the dogs—they had not stopped staring at me from the truck windows. As I fed the machine one bottle at a time, I had the opportunity to reflect on the old days when there were recycle clerks to count up our returns—five to ten minutes and bingo, you were out of there. I was feeling nostalgic, when the bottle machine jammed again. This had to be a conspiracy to convince people that it's too much trouble to recycle. I decided that when I got home I would write a letter to Homeland Security about this sinister plot. I checked the dogs and pushed the red button on the call box again. Seven more times the machine jammed on me. I was on a first-name basis with the clerk when I finally said, "To heck with it." I had a couple of dozen printouts of paper with my recycle count on them, some with as much as a five-can count.

The many bags of returns I had left, I offered to a guy who rode up on a bicycle. The rain wasn't stopping him from recycling. He gladly took my burden, and I ran into the store to cash out. Fifteen checkout stands and only three of them open, plus the four u-scan counters. Soon the checkout clerk will go the way of the recycle clerk. Won't that make shopping a joy? We all know how well those scanners work, and, of course, they always have the correct price. You bet. It was another ten minutes before I got my six dollars and twenty cents for my recycling efforts.

When I got back to my truck, all was lost. All that remained of the pizza was shredded cardboard and bits of plastic wrap. While cleaning up the mess, I kept asking the dogs, "How could you do this?" Of course, if they could talk they would say, "Very easy. You left the pizza right in front of us." Duh!

I couldn't help but notice that the guy I'd given my returns to wasn't having any trouble with the recycling machines. As I stopped by Papa Murphy's for my replacement pizza, I wondered if they sold antidepressants, too. The clerk said to me, "Hey, man, weren't you just in here? You must have the munchies!"

When we got home both dogs went to their food bowls to beg for dinner. I guess Tuesday and Utah did just what corporate CEOs do when you leave them unattended at the trough. They eat it all and expect you to refill it without complaint.

Chickens and Terrorist Dogs

My bride Sioux and I ordered twenty five-day-old chicks from Murray McMurray's catalog. The group consisted of Jersey Black Giants, Dark Cornish, and White Wyandottes. The date for their arrival was marked very clearly on our calendar. So I was rather shocked when the Medford Post Office called at 4:45 p.m. on a Sunday informing me that our chicks had arrived. "No," I replied, "they're not due for another six weeks." Needless to say, I hadn't remotely prepared for our baby chicks' arrival.

I raced to the Central Point Grange, which I knew would not be open, and sure enough, it had been closed for twenty-five minutes when I entered the empty parking lot. Driving around to the back of the store, I found Ken sitting on a picnic table waiting for his ride home. Climbing out of my manly Ram pick-up truck, I whined my "woe-is-me" chicken predicament—no feed and no electrolyte vitamins. "No problem," Ken smiled. He proceeded to fix me up with the supplies I needed. Ken is the Grange Co-op employee of the year in my book!

After arriving home with the peeping chicks, I quickly created an assembly of cardboard boxes using that magical invention—duct tape. This would serve as temporary housing for the chicks. I arranged the boxes on three of the dining room chairs, placed the chicks in their new digs, and turned on their heat lamp. Voila! All was okay with our new feathered friends.

Our Border Collies Tuesday and Utah loved hanging out in the dining room with the chicks. Tuesday wanted to sit on my lap with her head hanging over the side of the chick condo. She would sit and stare at the babies with her tongue hanging out. (That's her deep-thought look.) I had to explain to her that neither my lap nor my butt could endure this endeavor endlessly.

Several days later I had to venture to Grants Pass on errands. After a long day in town, it felt great to get back home. When I opened the door to the kitchen there were no dogs to greet me. Strange, I thought. They're always at the door upon my return.

Stepping into the kitchen, I was deluged with disaster. I couldn't believe my eyes. The chick condo was upended on the floor and ripped to shreds. The dining room chairs were flung every which way. The bottom pan drawer to the stove was in the middle of the kitchen floor. There was broken glass from the chick feeder scattered around and an empty one-gallon water container shoved into a corner. Wood shavings covered the entire kitchen, dining room, into the living room, down the hallway, extending into the bedroom, and onto our bed.

Good grief! We've been the victims of a terrorist attack. I knew I should have been raising pigs. That would have kept those terrorists at bay. No, our terrorists weren't from the Middle East, but rather they lived right here under our own roof. Tuesday and Utah were in hiding, and I just knew our chicks had been lunch for those two insurgents.

Then I heard a heavenly sound—little "peeps." The baby chicks were hiding under the shredded condo and behind some tins in a corner. Tuesday and Utah were cowering in the corner on the far side of the bed. I am sure my colorful language was heard all the way to Portland.

I proceeded to use a whole roll of duct tape (from my federal anti-terrorist survival kit) to assemble a new cardboard dwelling. This time it looked more like a pop-up camp trailer than a fancy condo. By now the exhausted chicks were very easy to round up, as Tuesday and Utah had spent the day herding them all around the house. How did I discover this? By playing Sherlock Holmes, I found a trail of little chick turds going from room to room.

I fired up our Hoover wind tunnel vacuum to start the clean-up. I was sucking up wood shavings from under the stove in order to put the pan drawer back in when I thought I saw some movement out of the corner of my eye. "Great," I thought, "I've uncovered a mouse nest." But no, it looked too big for that. Then I thought, "Holy moley, a rat." No, it was just one very traumatized little chick that had survived the dogs only to find itself being chased around by the vacuum cleaner hose from hell.

As I looked around the house, which resembled a nuclear test site, I couldn't believe that only one chick had died. It appeared that it was a casualty of being mashed by the overturned cardboard condo. Obviously, Tuesday's and Utah's intent had not been to eat the chicks, but rather to start their "training." That's right, instructing them in the proper procedures of being herded about.

I called Sioux at the San Francisco Veterans Hospital, where she was working the emergency room, and relayed the tale to her. She, logically, asked me why I hadn't left the dogs closed up in the back of the house like I had been doing. "Well, I, uh, uh . . ." was all I could come up with.

So what's the moral here? Border Collies will be Border Collies, and J.D. will be . . . well, let's not go there. Or maybe it's that when you think you have everything under control, it will spiral out of control in the blink of an eye. Kind of like the world at large.

*Tuesday spends hours staring at baby chickens
and hours herding them later in life, 2004*

The Boys, Utah. and Homeland Security

At 5:00 a.m., Uncle Sam found me standing bleary-eyed at the ticket counter check-in, with a wide yawn, at the Medford Airport. The ticket agent asked me for my photo ID or driver's license. I gave him my driver's license. Man, I needed more coffee. The ticket agent smiled as he entered my driver's license into his computer. Then his smile faded, and he excused himself, disappearing into the back room.

Four other people checked in at the next counter, while I fidgeted around for at least ten minutes, waiting for the ticket agent to reappear. When he finally did show up again, he said, "Sorry for the delay, sir." The mighty two-watt bulb in my head suddenly kicked in. I moaned inwardly, uh oh, there's some sort of asterisk by my name on his Homeland Security photo ID background checklist. Sioux had *said* she was going to turn me in to these guys if I didn't quit drinking Diet Pepsi, but I didn't think she really would. Nah, that couldn't be it—that's a small order of fries for these guys. They want the real thing.

Now, you may call me paranoid (a great song by Black Sabbath), but when the next Homeland Security agent emptied my suitcase and pawed his way through my belongings, I knew there was a red flag by my name. The only action missing was K-9 sniffing dogs, but I'm sure those guys in the back were most definitely S.W.A.T. disguised as baggage handlers.

I asked the highly trained Homeland Security agent if he wanted me to strip so he could check other secret hiding places on my person. He replied in an "Oh-I'm-so-bored" voice, "That won't be necessary." Of course, I regretted the question as the words spewed from my lips. What if the agent had said, "That's a good idea, Mr. Rogers. Please follow me to our sound-proof interrogation room." Once there, I might have been probed and prodded until my voice was several octaves higher. I'm sure I would have missed my flight by then.

Managing to clear the rest of the security checkpoints, I finished the first leg of my flight to Salt Lake

City via Phoenix. Sitting in my cramped window seat with the ill-fitting headrest, I pondered why there was a red flag by my name in the computer.

I was flying to Utah where I had once lived. I'm sure there are no outstanding arrest warrants against me and no moving violations in the last twenty-five years that I can remember. Maybe the powers-that-be knew I was meeting up with the "Utah Outlaws," who are notorious only in their own minds—that is, what's left of their minds from working in the mines. Although we were going to be completely debauched for the next eight days, we were going to be camped in the back country of the mighty La Sal Mountains, out there where the only possible victims could be ourselves. Besides that, the outlaws, whose faces were once known to most lawmen throughout the West, are now respectable pillars in their communities. Go figure, but it goes to show that in America anything is truly possible.

For many an evening during the next week, the conversation around our campfire centered on the cause of the trigger effect I experienced at the airport. Some thought that maybe Avon High School, which I attended in Indiana, was a hot spot for government dissent while I was in attendance. I pointed out that when I was at Avon High, we never achieved such honors, as we weren't even accredited. Study Hall and Shop were the only classes offered.

It was pointed out to me that I had worked in the uranium mines, but nothing is or was "top secret" in the mine. If I had stashed high-grade ore under my bed, surely I would have been taken out by cancer after so much time. Though the popular belief is that I glow in the dark, this glow may or may not be due to uranium mining.

Others thought some govern"mental" thought-police may have played one of my recordings backwards, discovering that people were being brainwashed with the repetitive phrase "Eat Miracle Whip." Yes, I do eat Miracle Whip, but all my recordings were done on cassette tape or CDs—neither of which plays backwards very easily.

No answers manifested themselves as we crawled around the La Sal Mountains under a "Utah Blue" sky with all the aspen trees turning to their brilliant gold fall colors. It's a good thing I took pictures so I would know where I'd been.

What about the return trip? I won't say what a guy might carry in his wallet that will set the Salt Lake City Airport Homeland Security Force into action, but I'll never carry one of those again!

It wouldn't surprise me if one day we find Homeland Security checkpoints going in and out of the Applegate Valley. Why? There are probably way too many potluck get-togethers with more desserts than is legal. Let it be known you won't find me eating desserts. No siree. Or maybe it's because in the Applegate there are folks left, right, and in the middle who actively speak out on issues. Actually, it will probably happen because we just have way too much fun out here.

What? Retirement Adjustments?

Our household has experienced a major change. One I consider *excellent,* and too long in coming. My sweet bride, Sioux, has retired from the Veterans' Administration Hospital in San Francisco as of January 31st. Sioux has been a nurse for forty-two years, the last fourteen as a commuting nurse to the VA Hospital. She would be gone for eight days and then home for six days, but her travel time between here and San Francisco came out of her six days off. Sioux also did pet-sitting while she was in the Bay Area (she missed our pets). This led to an occasional three or four weeks at a stretch of her being away from home, especially in the last two years. *But no more!*

A lot of friends have warned that we would have a readjustment period to wrangle through. I think our Border Collies, Tuesday in particular, have had the biggest adjustments to make. Tuesday always slept on Sioux's pillow when she was gone. When Sioux returned home the two of them would battle for the spot closest to me (it's nice to be fought over). Of course, it was Tuesday who went to the foot of the bed—ever so reluctantly—with her tongue hanging out about an inch. She would glare at Sioux, and we know she was thinking, "Soon Nurse Ratchet will be gone, and I'll be curled up by JD's head, cleaning his ears at will."

Utah has a sheepskin (fitting for a Border Collie) to sleep on the floor by Sioux's side of the bed, so he is trying to adjust to always being tripped over, stepped on, or, in the best case, stepped over. Anyway, he keeps getting awakened from his dreams of chasing birds from our feeders.

Tuesday always rides in the front passenger seat of my big Ram pickup truck. Now that Sioux has permanent residential claim to that seat, Tuesday has to ride in the back seat with Utah, who has been used to sprawling over four-fifths of the seat. He has been very reluctant to give up any of "his" area. So now, with her tongue sticking out, Tuesday glares at Sioux from her cramped spot in the back seat, thinking, "Soon Nurse Ratchet will be gone, and JD will be scratching my head instead of holding HER hand!" And so it goes in the readjusting Rogers' household.

As for me, I haven't had much adjustment to make, except for not having my ears cleaned nightly and not eating tomato soup straight from the can for dinner anymore. When Sioux and I met and I was the "Unknown Rock Star," she was my groupie, private nurse, and companion 24/7, and we got along splendidly, even when she'd threaten me with an enema bag after she'd cleaned our front yard and driveway of all the female fans and hangers-on who waited, panting, for the "Unknown Rock Star." She still has that bag, so I'm trying to stay on my best behavior.

Sioux is adjusting to retirement very easily. She has many hobbies and interests that keep her high-strung and busy—her triple A energy level humming right along. I know there will be some speed bumps along the way, such as Tuesday needing therapy to work through her "Soon Nurse Ratchet will be gone" issues. We hope that won't take too long. As for me—I'm sure glad you're home, Babe!

The Nurse, PTSD, and Cattle Guards

My bride and private nurse, Sioux, and I have just returned from a 3,000-mile road trip. We traveled to Colorado and Utah—Moab, Utah, in particular. This is the land of red rocks, blue sky, green Jell-O with Kool Whip, marshmallows, Yoohoos, and 3.2 beer. Yes, a visit to my homeland.

We traveled with our two Border Collies. Our *big* Ram pick-up was loaded with nine days of survival supplies: coffee and coffee maker. Heck, what else do you need? Well, Nurse Sioux added fruit and healthy snacks.

Tuesday rode on a pillow on top of our suitcase. From this throne, Queen Tuesday could stretch out, peek out any window and watch the sights as they flew by. Without moving she could clean my unsuspecting ears if they needed it—according to her, they always need it. That made for a lot of tongue dodging. Now, there's an idea for a new Olympic sport. The event could be called "wet ear" or "tongue the drum." I wouldn't want to go up against a St. Bernard or a Great Dane, though. Their tongues are the size of a Mack truck. Plus these dogs are big enough to pin you to the mat and just suck your eardrum and brain right out of your head. That wouldn't be a pretty sight, or a pleasant sound, for that matter.

Poor Utah! He didn't have his normal two-thirds of the back seat on which to sprawl as he usually does. He had to content himself by placing his rump high up on Tuesday's throne. That put him in a half sitting, half lying state for most of the trip.

The nurse and I always try to stay off the freeways as much as possible. If you really want to see the country, you have to travel the back roads.

Somewhere between Lakeview, Oregon, and Denio, Nevada, Utah leapt onto the front seat of the truck. He was shaking like a Florida hurricane was blowing on him and drooling like someone had left the irrigation ditch turned on maximum output. "Holy moley," I thought. "He must have eaten something at our last pit stop that poisoned him." Nurse Sioux looked at his gums and eye coloring and told me to relax, that he hadn't been poisoned. Something had really freaked him out.

I pulled off at the first wide spot in the road. I got Utah out of the truck, where Tuesday was already barking in his ear, "Mellow out, dude. All is well." By the time I found the paper towels among our survival gear in the back, Utah was wagging his tail. I wiped off the dashboard and the cup holders, all the while wondering how he could possibly have drooled so much in such a short period of time.

With the truck all wiped down and everyone back in their accustomed places, we continued on our journey. Fifteen minutes later we had a complete replay.

This time I figured our what caused it. Utah has a phobia about cattle guards. It must be that rat-a-tat-tat sound the tires make when crossing. The nurse delivered a diagnosis: "Utah has post traumatic stress syndrome or PTSD. The sound probably reminds him of gunshots. " It's great to have your own nurse traveling with you.

The rest of the trip consisted of driving sixty-nine mph, spotting a cattle guard, rapidly down-shifting, braking to make our crossing at a staggering three mph, while Sioux and I sang many versions of "La-la-la-la" very loudly and in different keys to distract the boy. Half the time we went through this process only to find the cattle guard was a fake—just white lines painted across the road. Of course, there were those we missed, and you can imagine what happened.

I can see where this PTSD can be a serious thing. When I think about it I realize I've got it, too. Whenever I go into a school (or even just think of one) or a hospital, I behave a little like Utah. I want to run away. I get the shakes and break into a profuse sweat. Luckily, I don't start drooling—at least, not yet.

The countryside was beautiful, with all the storms in the distance, the shadow lighting, and lots of wildlife. We saw mule deer, antelope, bald and golden eagles, and hundreds of cranes—the list could go on and on.

In Moab we hung with some of my old Utah outlaw buddies: Rickey Lee Costanza, Al "El Supremo" McLeod, and "Bad" Bob Ossana, and their families. They're definitely of the desperado type.

Rick took me, Sioux and our two dogs for a ride up to Castle Valley—one of the prettiest red rock valleys around. Long before developers hit that valley, we had used it for one of our many hideouts from local authorities. On this trip I had failed to mention to Rick anything about Utah's problem with cattle guards. Yikes! As we crossed one at ninety mph, Utah came over the front seat like a nuclear warhead. Chaos engulfed the truck cab. Utah shook like a flag in a gale wind, his eyes bulging with fear, his mouth foaming.

Rick held the steering wheel steady with one hand while reaching for his forty-five with the other. He thought Utah had gone mad, or, even worse, that he had rabies. While Nurse Sioux calmed Utah down (she has that effect on me, too), she explained to Rick that Utah has PTSD and cattle guards set him off. While Rick thought about this, Tuesday started in on his ears. Most folks try to get away from her at this point. Not Rick. "Good girl, Tuesday" and "That'a girl," were his comments. With that kind of encouragement Tuesday went into hyper-overdrive ear-cleaning mode. I pointed out to Sioux that Rick had breathed a lot of radon gas over the years, and this is the sorry aftermath.

When we left Moab for home I wanted to stop in Crescent Junction, Utah, and see if the Justice of the Peace was still around. I had gotten to know him well over the years, but it wasn't because we ran in the same social circles. These days Crescent Junction is like a lot of small towns across America—Mom and Pop stores are boarded up, factories are closed, many "For Sale" signs are seen along the main streets. Where has everyone gone?

We spent the night in Battle Mountain, Nevada. We pulled into a motel, as the weather had turned bad. The next morning, with snow on the ground and cold in the air, we prepared for the last leg of our trip.

I was at the front desk of the motel checking out while Sioux was loading our gear and the dogs into the truck. A freight train came rumbling by a short distance from the motel parking lot, with the usual "rat-a-tat-tat" sound coming from the train's wheels. Utah was out of the truck faster than you can say "pussy-cat." Sioux thought he was heading for the road to Reno, but, luckily, he stopped at the motel room door, frantically scratching to get in while shaking and drooling to beat the band.

Nurse Sioux calmed him down once again as the last train car finally rolled by. She loaded him into the truck one more time as I came out the door.

I guess many things can set off PTSD in an animal, just as in people. You don't know how it will manifest itself, but with help and understanding, you might be able to work through it all.

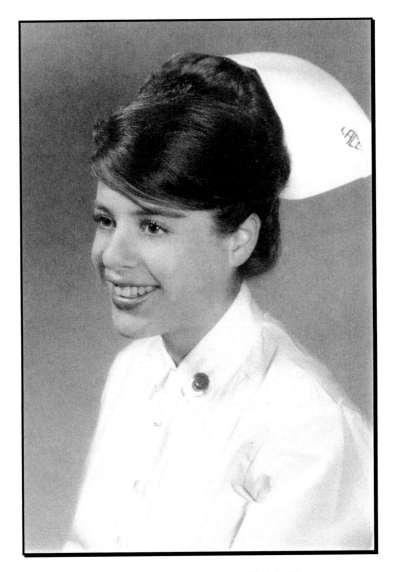

I just love it when my private nurse and bride Sioux wears her hat.

Grass Stains and Rock Bands

I was down at Eve's Cafe the other morning when some folks asked me if it were true what I had written about attending an unaccredited high school. It pleased me to know someone reads my column. I answered, "You bet!" and then proceeded to tell them all about Avon High, located in rural Avon, Indiana.

Though what I told them was politically incorrect, I didn't say this to put anyone down. It's just how it was, or seemed to me. I believe in those days Avon High was where the school district sent teachers who were mentally, physically, and academically challenged. The shop teacher, for example, had a wooden leg. Every year he would tell us a rearranged story about how he came by this peculiar appendage. The stories began with World War I and ended with a disastrous coal-mining accident. He could have easily been the leading character in *Grumpy Old Men*. He never smiled, except once when he cut off my wide tie (a fad at the time) with the hula girls on it at the Windsor knot. As I sat there with my Windsor knot, learning the skills of soldering, Mr. Shop Teacher informed me I was doing everything wrong. He then proceeded to demonstrate the methods of proper soldering. While he was engaged in this teaching activity, I noticed that his necktie was lying across the workbench, and at that moment I had a flash of genius. I engaged the trigger on my soldering gun and placed it on his tie as I politely answered, "I see, sir." When the stream of smoke from his burning tie reached his flaring nostrils, I was truly amazed at how quickly he jumped back from the table. With his 'holy' tie smoking, he yelled, "Rogers, you idiot!" He retired not too long after his wooden leg was removed from the shop closet and run through the wood lathe. Awesome designs.

Avon High had another infamous teacher with a glass eye. He would give you the "wrath of god" if he thought you were staring at it. Whether you were or were not staring was a moot point. You could still have a desk thrown at you.

The band instructor had only one arm. When the band played off key, which was most of the time, he would get so frantic that his arm stub would start to flail in the air.

The band students would then get so spooked, they couldn't look at him, at which point synchronicity could not have been bought at any price.

The science teacher was a classic, straight out of a B-movie. He dressed in a long stiff white lab coat, wore big black glasses, and did a constant "clank, clank, clank, clank" sound with marbles held hostage in the depths of his lab coat pocket. He seemed to like standing behind me particularly, going "clank, clank, clank, clank"--a sound as bad as fingernails on a black board. One day, one of my female classmates jumped up and asked him to *please stop!* He did, for just a moment, then back to the "clank, clank, clank, clank."

The guidance counselor cum chorus teacher looked like Wimpy from the Popeye cartoons, and thus earned his nickname. I always wondered why he was so friendly and personal with all the guys.

The principal was the dictator of dress codes and morality. He definitely did not like my cape collection or my suede boots. He thought jackets with elbow patches were the way one should be stylin'. Morality? He later ran off with the chorus teacher who had replaced Wimpy.

Surprise! We did have a few good teachers: the government, German, and French teachers. The French teacher, who was new, supervised my study hall. She was purported to be hot and drove a GTO that could snap your neck when you dumped the clutch. Ya, baby! I excelled in study hall.

For all my negative observations of Avon High, I must admit that high school gave me direction. I decided to be a football hero. The coach/history teacher was very cross-eyed. I could never tell when he was talking to me because his eyes were somewhere else. Anyhow, I made third-string defensive end. This, of course, meant my career was to be a bench warmer.

The sixth game of the season was in play. We had lost our first five games by an average of thirty-five points. In fact we had yet to score a touchdown. It was the fourth quarter, and the score was a grand forty-five to nothing. Avon High owned the "nothing." The coach was pacing up and down the bench while I was praying, "Please, please pick me. My jersey has never seen a real game grass stain."

Suddenly—"Rogers, in." I ran out on the field, all 6'4", 110 pounds of me. If I stood sideways and stuck out my tongue, I could have been mistaken for a zipper. My heart was bounding with overwhelming excitement. The referee had to yell, not once, but twice, "Twenty-four, you're offside, back up." Then the other team kicked off. I fell into blocking formation, then *pow*, I was hammered from the back, and down I went.

Suddenly, breathing was an overwhelming chore. Try as I would, I could not stand up. This was just great. Mom, Dad, and Grandfather were in the grandstands, I'd had my five seconds of football fame, got my first real game grass stain, and I couldn't move. The referee was standing over me.

"Twenty-four, you all right?"

The coach came over and said, "Rogers, quit dogging it!" Was he talking to me? His eyes were somewhere else.

As I was recovering from my fractured vertebrae, I realized I could play the guitar better than I could play football. I also decided during this protracted recovery that the girls liked me better playing guitar in a rock band than looking like a zipper wearing a football helmet. Anyhow, this is when I decided I was going to be a rock star, even if just an unknown rock star. Thus I give credit to the Avon High athletic department for giving me my musical direction.

Further encouragement came from the principal, wearing those patches on the elbows of his jacket, before he ran off with the chorus teacher. After one of our many dress code discussions, he candidly said, "Rogers, maybe it would be best for all concerned if you just drop out of school." I thought that was a nifty idea, but my parents would not have any of that. Much to the principal's chagrin, I plugged along and graduated from Avon High, rubber diploma in hand.

The point of this long and woeful tale is this: no matter where you come from, or how bad the odds or voices of discouragement may be, stick your fingers in both ears and don't listen to anyone but your own heart. Give your dreams your best shot, and win or lose, you'll know that you've tried.

JD's rock 'n roll headshot, 1986

Brownie Points

A little while back, Sioux was digging a hole in our ever-expanding garden to plant a two-gallon plant. This looked like a golden opportunity for yours truly to score some much-needed brownie points with the nurse. I'm always in dire need of points in the positive column, in hopes they'll cancel out all those marks in the Bad Boy column.

I boldly stepped forward and said, "Sweet love, let me dig that hole for you." I could see in her eyes that I was scoring some very big points with my offer. Sioux handed me the shovel, and I told her I would expand the diameter of the hole she had started so there would be more room for the plant's roots.

"Honey," I said, "after this plant is in the ground, would you like to pull up our rockers on the front porch? I'll pour us a glass of wine (Jim Beam for me), and we can gaze across our own gardens of Eden." Her response was, "I would be thrilled to sit with you." Boy, oh, boy, was I ever racking up the points now. Life was going to be excellent tonight.

I put all my oomph into the first stab with the shovel, thinking she would like my aggressiveness with the task for which I had so proudly volunteered. With a loud clank of metal shovel hitting on hard—very hard—rock, I let out a high-pitched squeal in an octave I didn't know I could reach. I fell to my knees, grabbing hold of my left wrist, which felt like a charge of TNT had just been set off in it. My arms were extended towards the heavens above. There was a very short vocabulary list screeching through my tightly clenched teeth.

Any neighbor who happened to be driving by at that point would have said, "Lookie there, JD's found religion. He appears to be praying or maybe speaking in tongues, from the way his body is quivering," as they hastily sped past.

My eyes were shut tight as the pain intensified, and I fell onto my side. From a fetal position on the ground, I whimpered in a weak, cracking voice, "I don't think I'll be digging the hole for you." Ahhhhhhhh.

Opening my eyes, I looked up at Sioux. She had both hands on her hips. Her lips were held tightly like she was going to kiss me, but I knew that wasn't going to happen. She had that look of disappointment on her face. Macho man rolling around on the ground had lost any brownie points he had hoped to collect. Possibly some points would even be added to the Bad Boy column.

Even Tuesday and Utah just sat there staring at me. I was sure they were thinking, "What a wimp! We dig holes all the time. All you had to do was ask, and we would have helped you. What a loser!" Then they up and abandoned me to go herd our chickens around. Much more entertaining.

The nurse escorted me into the house and had me sit down at the kitchen table. She then went into her ER mode. As she poked around on my wrist, she said that I might have an impact fracture. I let out a faint, whiny whimper at that diagnosis. She told me, "Hush, don't be a big baby, or you'll get an enema."

The kitchen became Sioux's M.A.S.H. unit, as she pulled out her medical supplies and put a posterior cast on my arm to immobilize my wrist. I'll tell you proudly that later the doctor was impressed with her cast job. That news made Sioux beam, knowing that she hadn't lost any of her ER skills since her retirement in February.

An x-ray later showed no broken bone. However, if anyone applied pressure to my wrist, old wimp boy would start thrashing around. The diagnosis was a sprained wrist. I was put out of commission, onto the disabled gardener list for four to six weeks. I had to cancel my summer plans—"The Unknown Rock Star Tour for 2005." That just totally bummed out fans in Gnaw Bone, Indiana; Tap Root, Kentucky, and Nitro, West Virginia. Well, maybe next year. As for brownie points, I think I'll just pick flowers for Sioux and tell her how much I love her. That's a heck of a lot less painful.

Sioux, JD and Boogie the day they made their move from LA to their ranch in Applegate, Oregon, 1988.

Remembering and Time

It's hard to believe that the holiday season is fast upon us. Another year has passed by at the speed of light. I'm told there were many, many things that happened in this passing year, but I don't remember many of those events, and that's probably a good thing.

There are advantages to not remembering things. For instance, when I get into trouble for doing something that's upsetting to my bride Sioux, I can convincingly say, "Are you sure I did that?" or "Why, I can't imagine doing something so stupid. Are you sure it was me?" or "Honey, you know I've killed a lot of brain cells over the years, but I'm certain I couldn't have done something as idiotic as that." Sometimes this works. But usually, I'm just in trouble.

As time and memory pass by, one thing stays constant—the never-ending "Honey Do" list. It never fades into the sunset, and there appears to be no ending to it. How could there be when the "Honey Do" list is expanding faster than our universe? Why, even Einstein couldn't come up with an equation to solve or explain the "Honey Do" list.

When I'm asked, "When are you going to do this or that thing?" I respond with "I'm getting to it." Only to be told that I've been saying that for ten years. "I have?" I question. "I don't remember that." And so it goes.

There are some things I remember quite well, like sitting at my desk at school watching the second hand on the clock over the door tick off the seconds ever so slowly. I still swear that it would slow down to the point that I thought it would never move again. While I was sitting there staring at the clock, an hour would feel like a lifetime, and a day became eternal. Same thing would happen if I had to stand in the corner, or if I'd been grounded for some infraction that to this day, I can't remember doing. But I do remember how long ten minutes, an hour, or a week was back then. I thought time was frozen in place and I would never see the end of it.

Now that I'm twenty-eight (well, maybe a little older), I am amazed at how fast time passes by. Yesterday was gone in a snap, and that was faster than the day before. I've figured out that if there is something you really want to do (that isn't on the "Honey Do" list), the best thing is to do it today, right now—not tomorrow, next week, next month, or next year. Just ask any of the folks who are in their "golden years." They'll tell you to climb those mountains, swim that ocean, and hike that continent while you are young.

I remember when this wisdom was branded into my brain. I was twenty years old. Doo Doo the Wonder Dog and I were living out of my car, with a trunk full of guitars and amps, at Lions Park in Moab, Utah. I met this old man who was traveling in a top-of-the-line motorhome. After an evening around the fire, he gave me what he said was the best advice he could give anyone. He said, "We run our lives backwards. We should do all of our adventure stuff when we're young. Then when you get old, like I am now, that's when you go to work. As you age, even if you're in good shape, you can't do things like a young person." I asked him what kind of things he was talking about. He said, "I can't climb a mountain, but you can." That's the best sermon I ever heard.

Remembering his words, I followed that path for many years, whether I was living in the mountains or rockin' on stage. I tried to live that philosophy the best I could. Now the one troubling thing is that even though I try as hard as I can, I can't remember that old guy's name. And he was the only teacher who ever truly influenced me.

Other things I try to remember to do are to tell my bride and family that I love them, hug our dogs, keep old friendships new, hope our new ones become old, and laugh and laugh a lot—remember, life is good.

If there are any other thoughts, I don't remember them. Oh yes, time is short!

J. Michael Pearce, JD Rogers, and Al "El Supremo" McLeod somewhere in southeastern Utah, 1985

Sioux at our wedding reception in Silver Lake, Ca, 1988

Oh, Litter Boy! Or We Are Tourist

I'm writing this from Los Angeles, California. I haven't been into the belly of this beast in over a decade. Some things down here haven't changed since my last exhausting, mind-boggling visit. The Rainbow Club, The Roxy, and The Whiskey are still rockin'. It's good to know there are still some hard-core "hair" rockers that are coming up through the ranks.

There is little visible smog. I have been able to see Mt. Wilson every day. There must be some sort of wind pattern, or maybe some government climate control operation, that is responsible for this rare air quality. Why? All the freeways have more cars and trucks than ever, all moving at breakneck speeds of eleven miles per hour. That kind of G-force doesn't pull your lips back over the top of your head. They just hang limp as one mutters the unspeakable about these beastly roadways. There is also the never-ending noise factor: helicopters circling endlessly twenty-four hours a day, a continuous roar from the freeway, and the background irritant of barking dogs, car alarms, screams, gunshots, televisions, radios, boom boxes, grinding metal, screeching tires, voices, voices, voices loud and soft, and dying last breaths. In all fairness, there are a few architectural gems remaining, but they're hard to find, hiding amongst the graffiti. The rest of the stucco and plaster has an unnatural bonding with old ivy or morning glories. This is all rather unnerving for one who is accustomed to the serenity and quiet hum of Applegate, Oregon.

Los Angeles doesn't have a night sky. Sioux was sure she was looking at her favorite harvest moon. I had to break the sad news to her that it was only a Shell gas station sign. It's never truly dark in a world of mercury vapor lighting. I spent one evening down here watching what has replaced shooting stars and constellations. It was a skyway of jet airliners as far as I could see into the distant horizon of an L.A. night, a parade of airplane lights coming and going from nowhere to everywhere.

You might be wondering why this unknown rock star is down here drowning in this sea of people. No, it is not to pick up my Grammy Award—that event is not for a few months. Sioux and I and our two Bordie Collies are on vacation. *We are tourists!* Yep. We are rubberbecking, without gray matter between our ears. We are those country hicks standing on the corner of Hollywood and Vine.

"Sioux, were those people honking and saluting us?"

We're actually visiting our son, Weston, and daughter-in-law, Monika. Utah loves the L.A. sun. Every afternoon we find him working on his dog tan. Tuesday, on the other hand, is freaked out by the noise and spends as much time as she can with her head buried 'neath a pillow. She is not sure about this big-city stuff. Weston and Monika have a cat named Kahlua and a dog named Bailey. Kahlua has Weston trained rather well. She meows, "Oh, litter boy. Change my cat box! Meow. Oh, litter boy, I'll be having dinner in bed." Bailey was saved from the dog pound. Weston wanted a large wrestling-partner dog like a Rottweiler. Monika wanted a large dog, too, like a Chocolate Lab. They were hoping for a mix of the two. The day they called the animal shelter they were joyfully told, "You folks are in luck. This morning we just rescued a Rottweiler/Lab-mix puppy. Weston and Monika raced down to the shelter and picked up their new addition to the family. A year later now, Bailey stands about ten inches high at her shoulders. She is definitely a mix all right. Chihuahua eyes, Cocker Spaniel ears, King Charles tail, long prancing legs, and an adorable face. They love their dwarf make-believe Rottweiller—Lab mix very much.

My favorite night down here was after a return from Venice Beach, still the hangout of all the characters from the first Star Wars bar scene. As we drove up to the kids' house, their side of the street was in a total blackout. The other side of the street had the god of electricity smiling on them. Was there a terrorist attack on our side of the street? Darn, I forgot to check and see what color the official government terrorist danger alert was. Well, out came the many well-used candles, and we all decided to play "dictionary." While we cleared off the table for the game, Weston went into the backyard to get or do something. In a flash he was back in the house, hopping around on one leg. The bare foot he was holding in the air had encountered what we call "doggie land mines." Yep, right between the toes. Weston was definitely on a roll. This was the third misplaced step in one day: one in his shoes, one in his socks, and this classic, my favorite, in his bare feet.

Playing dictionary was a hoot. Monika wrote all her definitions in her Czech accent; Sioux's all had to do with medicine or plants; Weston's were all food or drink-related, and mine...who knows. I can barely spell "JD." We were laughing until tears were rolling down all our cheeks and our sides ached.

Suddenly the miniature Rottweiler decided it was time to recycle dinner. After a nasty clean-up, we resumed playing, when Kahlua meowed: "Oh litter boy, I am bulimic, so look out." Sioux grabbed a good china bowl and made a partial save, and "litter boy" had less work to do that time. We had resumed playing when Kahlua meowed, "Litter boy, I've got a hairball, gag, gag."

After all the commotion, Weston thought that maybe if we played candlelight poker we might see a change in animal behavior, meow. Sioux had never played poker; Monika had played once; I am familiar with the game, and Weston was stoked as he pulled out his new poker chips for their maiden game.The short of it was, Sioux kept asking, "Are five clubs in consecutive numbers good? *Winner!*"

"Are three queens and two jacks a good hand?" *Winner!* She could not understand, as we pushed the mound of chips toward her, why the rest of us suddenly felt like we, too, needed a litter boy. So the game went on, as Monika put Weston out of play, gave him some of her chips, then proceeded to dispose of him again, and me a few moments later. The rookies went at it for quite some time, while Weston and I tried to give advice. The ladies pointed out that, since they were still playing, we were the losers, and they needed no advice. Monika wound up top dog of thenight.

This visit to the big city has been delightful, because I don't have to live here. I did utterly and thoroughly enjoy the chaotic comings and goings while I *calmly* ate six donuts at Tang's, my favorite donut store from twenty years ago, or had breakfast at Philippi's, where coffee is still ten cents a cup, and a refill is ten cents. Weston and Monika master-minded a dim sum brunch: Ordered in fast motion, eaten in faster motion, and most likely filmed on a Hollywood backlit set in Chinese fast motion.

But I can't wait to get home to the gentle quiet and soothing peace of my apple trees in the Applegate. I am told that L.A. was once lush and beautiful, filled with orange groves, avocado groves, strawberry fields, flower fields, and farms of every type. The famous "Farmer's Market" was really just that: the farmers brought their fresh produce to a central location, and the produce and flowers were sold directly off the carts. The sky was always blue, and seeing Mt. Wilson wasn't a rarity, but the norm.

I wonder, as southern Oregon, the Rogue Valley, and the Applegate, in particular, grow and grow, how long before we think back to how beautiful and magnificent this place was? I wonder, as our valleys are transformed into a land of concrete, tract houses, box stores, noise, and graffiti, do we realize what we are losing?

Nein English or Say What?

You'll never guess where I just did time. No, not in San Quentin or Susanville. I was back down in L.A. After a ten-year absence, I've been there twice in three months. Yes, sir, I've got nerves of aluminum!

My bride, Sioux, and I had an uneventful twelve-hour drive until we hit Burbank. That's where all six—or was it eight?—southbound lanes on I-5 came to a thundering halt. As we sat staring at taillights, I turned on a talk radio show. I rarely listen to wacky-hack, IQ of the dead, right-wing Lush Limpballs or left wing Foul Skankin-type radio. I go for the wack-a-boom shows, and we listened to a great one. The airway was awash in the sniveling ranting from a junior cadet from a nearby academy. This kid was totally amped up because eBay had the "bloody nerve" to close down an auction site that had posted an Iraqi insurgent's very dead skull for bidding action. This cadet said he was going to be the high bidder. He planned to hang the skull from his rifle to "psych out the enemy." Plan #2 was to just keep the skull in his room as a memento.

As I was laughing at this certifiable wacko, I spied two coils of what appeared to be choice ropes lying ahead of us on the freeway's worn asphalt. I pointed the ropes out to Sioux, and she asked, "Do you want me to go get them?"

"I don't think so, baby. The traffic might start moving again."

With that, Sioux bailed from the truck, dragged both large coils of rope and hoisted them into the truck bed. Tuesday and Utah, who had been asleep, were now quite frantically watching Mom out on the freeway. They both had a dumbfounded expression reading, "Whoa, didn't you two teach us not to play in traffic?" Good grief, the cars were starting to move just as Sioux returned to the safety of the big Ram pickup. As we crept along at the speed of a slug, cars crawled by trying to catch a glimpse of the crazy woman who had been playing rope relay on the freeway.

We had gone down to the City of the Angels for the ninety-fifth birthday of Sioux's father, David. He's in better shape than some forty-year-olds I know. He still has his own apartment, reads the classics and current events, likes a little Scotch, and is planning a trip to Ireland this spring. It was great to see, at the party, family and friends that we hadn't seen in some time.

My Utah outlaw buddy, J. Michael Pearce, formerly of the J. Michael Pearce Band, rode his rocket into town from Santa Fe, N.M. You may have heard some of his hit singles such as, "Colonoscopy Wall Climber" or "Impacted Wisdom Tooth Blues." J. Michael, Sioux, and I spent a day right in the middle of downtown L.A., studying architecture, language, and street people. I was standing on Broadway between Second and Third Streets, when this person wearing a bright blue jacket stained with every imaginable substance known to man, the whites of his eyes red, redder, and very red, smiled at me with his rotting, moldy, fungus-covered teeth. He asked, "Hey, brother, you got some change?" I was pretty sure we weren't related, so I replied, "Nein English." His response was, "You know, man—change." He rubbed his thumb over the inside of his finger, just inches from my nose.

"Nein English," I repeated. He thought for a moment (or was shorting out, I'm not sure which) and pulled some coins from his own pocket. "Hey, man, change, like this." I reached for the money, saying, "Danke, danke," but he quickly wrapped his crusty fingers around the coins and said, "No, man, you give *me* the change. Are you crazy?"

I said "Nein English" again as my new best friend staggered away down the sidewalk. The air around me lingered stale with the stench of Thunderbird or Mad Dog or Tokay wine, live from L.A.

For me, this outing was much needed. The night before we left Applegate, my doctor called with some lab reports.

"Say what?" I said to my doctor. "We must have a bad connection."

So I banged the phone on the table a few times, and asked him to say it again. He did.. He said I had prostate cancer. I felt like I had been kicked in the stomach. It was hard to breathe. I think I said something stupid like, "Okay, thanks," and hung up the phone.

A few weeks earlier during a routine blood test, my private nurse, Sioux, had suggested I have a PSA check, since it had not been done for several years. I had no symptoms of prostate problems. Test results revealed a PSA reading of 13.65. That's good, right? *Wrong!* Normal PSA level is 2.5 or below. Since there is often a "false positive" with this test, a prostate biopsy gives a definitive diagnosis. That was what the doctor had called me about. I flunked. On a scale of one to ten, ten being the worst, I was an unlucky seven. Maybe seven being "lucky" needs to be reevaluated.

So guys, here is my new sermon. Even if your man parts feel absolutely fine but you are over forty-five, get a PSA blood test. An early catch is a very doable cancer cure. If you have a family history of prostate cancer, get a PSA test at age forty.

By the time you read this column, I will be finished with surgery, lying in my own sweet bed and having my private nurse caring for my every need. I've met the grim reaper many times in my life, but always by surprise. On this one, I've had time to ponder what's important, what's not. Most of the day-by-day stuff is *not*. Watching rain drops collect into gullies *is*. Worrying about bills is *not*. Listening to the roar of the creek *is*. Wondering if my socks match my tee shirt is *not*. The things that really matter are watching the wild turkeys, studying a Jim Beam label, walking in the orchard with the dogs, and having Sioux hold my hand and say, "How ya doing, sweetheart? Remember those bulbs I planted late last season? Honey, look out the window. They're all blooming."

Sioux and JD in Price, Utah, for the funeral of Holiday Gang member Ken Hoffman.

Fashion Statement or Hollywood Weirdo

Sweet kisses from my bride and private nurse, Sioux, greeted me as I awoke from a deep fog. My prostatectomy, due to cancer, was done. Those heavenly kisses were quickly overshadowed by pain. I mean *real pain*. The up side of pain, if there is one, was that I was given a button to push every ten minutes for a squirt of morphine. After the floor nurse noticed I was pushing the button every thirty seconds while whining and moaning, I was given a reprieve and allowed a button push every six minutes. Life was definitely better being lost in a hallucinogenic dream without pain.

Nurse Sioux had slipped my green Converse high-top tennis shoes on my cold feet. Is that what all the doctors were laughing about? Maybe they were just laughing because my green feet hung over the edge of the bed. Did they really ask me if I played basketball for Notre Dame? I'm not sure if I answered with a giggle or a moan, or if they were even talking to me at all. I do for sure remember a few things. Sioux never left my side and slept in a chair next to me. At one point, though, she put her face right close to me. I thought I was going to get a sweet kiss again. Instead she said, very sternly, "Honey, I am going to the bathroom. I will be right back. If a medicine nurse comes in, or any one, and wants to put anything in your mouth, clamp it closed tight! Do you understand me?" I think I nodded in the affirmative, but she was not satisfied. I had to repeat the instructions verbally. She then left the room, yellow note pad clutched in her hand. I wonder if a thermometer was part of the code. I didn't get that clarified. Oh well, she was back by my side in a flash, standing as a protective guard against unforeseen errors.

On day three of my internment at the Norris Cancer Institute in Los Angeles, Sioux sprang me loose. I was loaded into our truck, and we drove a short ten minutes to recoup at the house of our son and daughter-in-law, Weston and Monika. Our kids had been taking care of our other "kids," our Border Collies Tuesday and Utah. If our two weren't enough, they had the ten-inch wanna-be Chocolate Lab/Rottweiler Bailey and a new seven-month-old puppy, Vega. Vega is from the same shelter as Bailey and with the same credentials. The shelter that called and said, "Hurry on down. We have another Rottweiler/Chocolate Lab puppy." Since Vega towers over Bailey, it seems as though the shelter was a little more on target this time. Their old cat, Kahlua, the one who meows, "Oh, litter boy," to Weston, sat and watched, with swishing tail and ever-stalking eyes, the four dogs running through the house.

I needed to get my strength back. Endless laps around the living room, while carrying my bag, was the exercise of choice. My bag was not filled with candy, dirty laundry, or groceries, but rather yellow liquid. I had had a Foley catheter installed during surgery. My "road map" incision was very tender, and I could not even bear to wear sweat pants. Weston to the rescue! He said I could wear his "skirt." *Say what!?* He kindly explained it was purple with black stars and fringe, a sarong, a long piece of fabric you just wrap around yourself. So there I was, being draped by

Weston in a long wrap-around skirt. Hey, whatever you call it, it looks like a *skirt*..Weston, do we need to talk? But it did the trick. I was comfortable and had a place to hang my "Gucci" bag, as Sioux called it. I think she thought I would feel more uptown with a designer bag.

There I was, doing living room laps, bent at a thirty-five-degree angle, wearing a skirt, my "Don't be a Dick" t-shirt from friend Hal Macy, and barefoot. I thought I might have a nose bleed as I was cruising at the speed of a very old Oregon banana slug. The ever faithful Tuesday was escorting me. I had navigated about twenty feet when I let out a scream. Nurse Sioux dashed to my side as she thought I had ruptured the embroidery. Nope, it was a very straight, straight pin going right into my left foot. As I hobbled around, searching for a landing spot to extract the pin, Tuesday started barking and jumping up on me. Was she trying to rescue me from the straight pin mishap? No, she thought I had come up with a new game to rescue her from her boredom. As I yelled at her not to jump on a one-footed man hopping around, I landed on another straight pin, straight into my right foot. I collapsed on the couch, while uttering a few French expletives, and removed both weapons from my feet.

On day seven of my living room tracking, Sioux said she was going to Home Depot to buy seedlings for the kids' garden.

"I want to go," I meekly said. That look of concern came over Sioux's face. It was the same look I had seen often.

"Are you sure?"

"Oh, yeah. It'll be fun and we'll have a good laugh." So we both piled into the truck, me sporting my green high-tops, long skirt, "UnderDog" t-shirt, and, of course, my Gucci bag draped at my waist. Sioux was wearing a look of grave concern again. I hobbled through the store, doing my Oregon banana slug crawl. Not one person looked at me. No one smiled, laughed, turned their head away, offered me a handicap place in line, or asked for my autograph. What a bummer! I obviously was mistaken for a common Hollywood home-boy weirdo.

The day finally arrived when I decided I could handle the ride back home to Applegate. Sioux did the truck driving, while I did the complaining about the millions of bumps on I-5. Even with the wonders of modern medicine—pain pills—we had to make at least twenty rest stops. Real rest stops for me to rest. Redding, California, was it for me. Sioux settled all of us into a motel room, unfortunately on the second floor because the first floor was full. Stairs were not an exciting prospect, but I could not travel farther.

We weren't in the room but a few minutes when all heck cut loose. What was that smell? Oh my God, poor little Tuesday had gotten sick with diarrhea. She was very bummed out (as were we), because she doesn't do that sort of thing indoors, unless it is a surprise. It was. Sioux headed to the store for cleaning supplies and diarrhea medication. I took Tuesday and Utah for a walk. For the next several hours Sioux and I traded taking the sick girl outside.

The night seemed to be settling down and the lights were dimmed, as we welcomed some much-needed sleep. Well, not much sleep. Heck, no. I heard Tuesday at the door, and Sioux was snoring. I got up like the wind of a played-out hurricane, all the while whispering, "Hang on, Tuesday. I just have to jump into my skirt and my green high-top tennis shoes and drape my bag." Tuesday had a sad look in her eyes. I knew what that meant. I was too late. Why didn't I just let her out, and then follow in my formal attire? Good question. As morning came around, and we were leaving the motel room, I looked around.

"Gosh Sioux, the carpet looks cleaner than when we arrived." No kidding!

It sure felt good to be back home in the Applegate. I truly love this place. While sitting on the porch, trying to catch some sparse rays of sun, I got to thinking how lucky I was that Sioux suggested I have a PSA test. I had had absolutely no symptoms of prostate problems. My prostate cancer was caught early enough that removal of my prostate was all I needed. I don't need radiation or chemotherapy, just a recheck on my PSA level every six months for the next five years. After that, once a year is enough, just like all of us (men that is) should routinely be doing anyhow.

Cancer is a very scary thing. To keep myself from becoming a wack-a-boom, I developed a more warped sense of humor than I already have. Laughing is so therapeutic. Hey, I had to wear a dribble pad for a long time, but there was no reason to whine about this chapter in my life. It wouldn't change a thing. Going to Bi-Mart was most entertaining. I would ask in a very loud voice, making sure all around could hear me, "My Great Great Grandpa needs disposable diapers. How do I know what size to get him?" The clerk asked me Great Great Grandpa's waist size. I said he is about the same as me, a thirty-six. She looked at me with a kind smile and said, "You'll do just fine with these," and handed me a medium. Then when all the folks around me started staring, I said, "I know, I know, but my Mom says this is the month I will finally be potty trained." And so it goes.

With family, friends, neighbors, well wishes from strangers, and lots of humor, this experience has had a positive twist. I now realize I have been able to do things that I would have thought impossible. I can laugh and not complain. I can wear a skirt, green high-tops, and an inside-out Gucci bag, and make a real fashion statement. As for Ms. Tuesday, she must have had a dreadful thirty-six-hour doggie bug. She held her head high with a sense of dignity and never complained either.

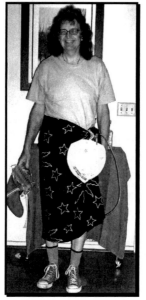

JD with his Gucci bag after prostate cancer surgery, 2006

Red Rock Addiction or Doing a Good Deed

I think I will just switch gears to the positive for this issue of the *Applegator* and recount my escapade back to my homeland, Moab, in southeast Utah, land of the red rocks, arches, natural bridges, balanced rocks, and goofy tourists, myself now included. "Medic" Bill Dunlap, my local Applegate buddy, went with me for his maiden voyage into the fog of no return known as Red Rock addiction. We hung out with a few of Utah's more notorious outlaws--Rickey Lee Costanza, Robert "Bad Bob" Ossana, and former Grand County (Utah) Commissioner Al "El Supremo" McLeod.

We haunted such places as Sego—Utah's crumbling ghost town—and Sinbad Valley, where it's so quiet not even a coyote, raven, or rattlesnake could be heard. Eleven glorious days of total debauchalism (if that is a word). No newspapers, radio, or television to distract us from the mystic, surreal colors of turquoise, purple, red, and orange from the setting sun. It was just us, our campfire, spiked coffee, tarantulas, scorpions, and buzzards. Ah, yes, very relaxing!

Our expedition into the Book Cliffs above Thompson, Utah, took us through some of the most rugged country in the lower forty-eight states. This is an area cursed with tar sands, oil shale, and natural gas. (Although my bride Sioux says I did not need to go to Utah for the last item.) The bankers, commodity traders, and developers will be here soon, but for a while we had a private world of our own.

Traveling through Doug firs, ponderosa pines, and aspens, we came upon an unknown black object lying by the side of the road Bad Bob thought it was an old bear. Medic Bill was sure it was an old tire. Slowly "it" lifted its head and looked cautiously at us as we approached.

"By golly, it's a dog," I said. The dog tried to stand, but was too wobbly on its first attempt. We stopped and piled out of the rig to give this poor wretched fellow a hand. He was very emaciated and dehydrated, and his right rear leg had been chewed on by coyotes. We gave him some water and a slice of bread and steadied him as he drank deeply.

"Not too much at one time," Medic Bill informed him. I could tell by his collar he was a hunting dog. Riveted into it was a large brass tag with his owner's name, address, and phone number—the best type of tag to have for dogs.

No camping out that night, as our newfound friend needed his wounds cleaned up. We loaded him into my Big Ram truck and headed for Moab. It was easy to quickly spoil our new traveling companion. He had three sets of hands petting and talking to him at all times. Two hours later, Bad Bob had called the dog's owner, who was coming the next morning from Desseret, a town in western Utah, to pick up his dog, Comet.

We were never even close to guessing his name. Comet had been part of a bear-hunting outing and had been lost for thirteen days. After some more food and water, he was a little more stable on his feet and wanted to walk around a bit, marking trees. That was a good sign--his kidneys were working. Bad Bob's daughter, Autumn, was able to raise a vet by phone, and she gave us instructions on what to do. Autumn cleaned up the wounds, and Comet was ready for a good night's sleep–full belly, no coyotes, bears, or chipmunks to worry about.

The next morning when Comet's owner showed up, the dog didn't seem too excited to see him, not even with a badly docked tail wag. Maybe we spoiled Comet with so much attention, good food, and riding in the cab of the truck, that he wasn't excited about going back to his old life. After we were assured that Comet wasn't going to be put down because of his leg wounds (Medic Bill asked the guy three times before he even knew his name), we headed for the Book Cliffs and another adventure. Comet headed home. When we were offered money for our trouble, which it wasn't, we told Comet's owner to just pass the good deed along.

Creatures from Hell or Huge Hairball

The other day, in the middle of a ghastly heat wave, I was tending to the new heirloom apple trees that grace our heritage orchard. Names like Victoria Limbertwig, Kentucky Limbertwig, Lowery, Hunge (my favorite), and Red Rebel, to name a few, remind me of a gathering of elite

Southern gentlemen. I was hot, sweaty, and grimy, and all I could think about was a nice cool shower.

I was halfway to the house when my bride, Sioux, shouted, "Honey, there is something dreadfully wrong with Tuesday. She's running back and forth and then in circles like a race horse." Little Miss Tuesday was by then running full speed ahead toward the house and then back toward me. In between, she would throw herself to the ground, bite her foot and her underneath private parts, and then take off for the racetrack again. I called her to me and, as she desperately tried to hold still, inspected her for an imbedded foxtail or some other irritant. I could find nothing wrong, and I was pretty sure that Tuesday was not changing occupations at her age from herder to trying out for the next Kentucky Derby.

I took her into the house with me. As I headed for the shower, she pushed herself in front of me and jumped into the bathtub. This was very curious, as this happens only when she knows I am going to hose her down after she has encountered some god awful smelling, decaying, nauseating, rotting mess of who knows what. But Tuesday did not stink, so I figured she just wanted a cool shower, too. As I stripped, she paced the tub, looking at me from around the shower curtain. I told her I was hurrying, but sweaty clothes stick to the body and mine were slow in peeling off. Finally, I threw a towel over the shower curtain rod, set the water temperature, and hopped in. I took the showerhead on the long hose, used especially for doggies, and set it on gentle shower. I know you are thinking that maybe there is some sort of perversion going on here. So, before you call "Pets With Pervert Owners" or some other group, let me say this: It is far easier to bathe our dogs with all of us in the shower than having a tidal wave on the ceiling, walls, and floor. I get soaked either way.

I began running the water on her underside and back to her flanks, telling her how good she was at training me to grant her every wish. With my right hand combing through the long hair on her underside, what had been tormenting her was suddenly freed, but still wanting vengeance. Tuesday bailed out of the tub, leaving me to fend for myself against a pair of zooming, bombarding creatures from hell. I tried to defend myself with a flow of shower water that was as powerful as a drip irrigation emitter.

"HORNETS," I shouted, as if someone would hear me. I grabbed the towel and gave a hard left with it, taking out one of the hellion suicide attackers splat against the wall. Not knowing where the second attacker was hiding, I made a dripping break for the bathroom door, tearing the shower curtain from most of its rings. Tuesday was now jumping up and down at the closed door. *Bummer!* I usually leave it open. I grabbed another towel from the rack, just as that little twisted demon varmint missed my forehead by a gnat's butt. Then I thought, "I am not going to let some three-quarter-inch half-pint without a flying license run me out of my bathroom!"

I looked at Tuesday and said, "It's you and me to the end, baby." Tuesday was now scratching at the solid wood door wanting "Out, please." She may have been thinking this is not the time to play Dirty Harry or to pretend you are Steven Segal. I was going to make Ice-T, 50 Cent, and all the other home boys in the 'hood proud. I turned to face my enemy head on.

"Come on, you miserable flying Freddie Krueger of a pest." He wasn't buzzing any more but had landed on an old industrial yarn spool on the very *top* of our medicine cabinet. If only I could make out his eyes. But I didn't have my glasses on, so I just gave him the old "Clint squint." We stared at each other.

"You wanna play tough? I'll pull a Mike Tyson and chew your wing off if you fly at me again." I gave the towel a little flip, making a cracking sound. I'm tough! Mr. Hornet slunk into a dry flower arrangement next to the old yarn spool. I opened the door, never taking my eyes off the menacing fiend, and Tuesday about knocked me down as she scrambled through my legs and out of the bathroom. So much for the tough-guy exit, as I grabbed the side of the door to keep from falling. Now all I had to do was explain to Sioux why I left a kamikaze pilot alive in the bathroom.

Tuesday fared well from the hornet attack. Next day, an early morning reconnaissance mission found Butch the Hornet up on top of the medicine cabinet, on his back with his wings up (maybe I scared him to death)!

A few days later Sioux informed me something was weird with our "niece," the beautiful long-haired calico cat, Chloe. This is the same cat we have been "babysitting" for two years while our nephew, Jeremy, is in Israel studying for his Master's degree. Sioux said Chloe has a *huge* hairball on her belly, and it felt soft and mushy on the inside. Not your typical hairball! Sioux was sure there was an entire blood-sucking tick family inside this hairball. I looked at it, gave this hairball thing a feel and said, "That ain't no tick, darling. I don't know if ticks could be that big even in the Amazon rain forest." I decided it might be a tumor.

We began doing removal surgery after a joint decision that I could be the surgeon and Nurse Sioux my assistant. I tried to get her to wear her nurse cap, but she refused, scowling, "I remember what happened the last time I wore that hat. No way, Buddy." Good try, but she still had to hold the screaming "patient" while I did surgery with delicate manicure scissors. Sioux held Chloe tightly and close to her, while I slowly cut the hairball loose.

"This is the worst thing I have ever felt," I said as I was cutting. Suddenly Chloe let out a blood-curdling scream, and I shuddered and said to the scrub nurse, "See, I told you it was a tumor." The nurse informed me I was doing my surgery too close to the skin.

"*Continue!*" she ordered.

Good surgeons always take orders from the head scrub nurse, so I continued. I was about three-quarters of the way through the hair mat when--POP! I dropped the scissors with a scream. I felt like I was in the dinner scene from the movie *Alien*. A three-inch banana slug, very alive and alert, came at me like a jack-in-the-box. Have you ever heard of a banana slug getting tangled up in the long hair of a cat, and then acting like a normal hairball? Damn imposter.

This weak-kneed boy finally recovered from the fright. Nurse Sioux remained calm. She is rarely grossed out after her many years in the emergency room, not to mention all the years she's had to live with my odd habits.

Two dramas in a couple of days are enough for me. Now I am preparing for more attacks from these types of terrorist cells in the near future. The alert level has been raised to orange at the Rogers household.

Bentley and Tuesday snuggling on a cold winter's day, 1999

A Car for a Song or To Use or Not to Use

"Welcome to Nashville, the country music capital of the world. We have blue skies with a temperature of

Blah, blah, blah. Thus ended another miserable—as always--airline flight. But, hey, I did make it to my destination of choice without running afoul of the highly trained air marshals, without becoming ill from that food-like "airline cuisine" served in a flimsy cardboard box; and without being forced to jump from the flying cattle car at 30,000 feet without the benefit of a parachute for some infraction I committed while watching an airline-selected soap opera on my nonworking airline headset. A very lucky trip, indeed!

I was in Nashville to meet up with J. Michael Pearce (formerly of the J. Michael Pearce Band) and new country music rising star Bill Todd. We were going to spend the next week pitching a Rolls Royce-worth of new songs we had written. We'd be spending time with a group of hyenas also known as music publishers. Most of this talentless collection of folks has never written a song themselves, but feed on songwriters' hard work. Yes, they'll give you a "Songwriter's Contract," but I do believe confederate dollars are worth more these days.

J. Michael met me at the deplaning corral chute, where he could see I was in need of immediate decompressing. He said, "Let's go to the Red Carpet lounge. Our good buddy Jim Beam is waiting there for us." Old Jim let it be known that he'd stay with us day and night as we tramped and crawled up, down, and all around Music Row. What a friend!

We decided to take care of our rental car, seeing as how our publishers hadn't seen fit to provide us with twenty-four-hour limo service. J. Michael said he'd seen a sign earlier at Budget car rentals that read "A Car for a Song." When we stepped up to the Budget rental counter, a very, very lovely lady, whose name tag read "Annette," said, "Welcome to Budget. How might I help you?" That's a loaded question for such a beauty to ask the likes of me. So I say, "Hi, Annette. Your sign there says 'A Car for a Song,' so if I sing to you, I get a car at no charge, right?"

Annette was flustered. "Oh, my God, no one has ever asked me that before! Oh, you guys are famous, I know you're with that band, um…, oh, my God, I love your pink Converses!"

"Why, thank you, Annette, but please don't say 'famous' too loud; we're trying to keep a low profile. You understand? About your sign, would you ask your manager about our inquiry?"

Annette returned a few minutes later with her manager, who also thought we were from a famous band. Mr. Manager said that no one had ever asked whether they'd get a free car if they sang.

"Mr. Manager, *we're* asking, so what do you say?"

"Well, that's what the sign says so, okay, we'll do it."

I said, "Man, that is great. As soon as our partner Bill Todd arrives, we'll give you a show."

We were back in half an hour. As Bill pulled his guitar from its case, and put his harmonica holder with a c-harp around his neck, a crowd started gathering around us. One girl in the crowd said, "I know these guys. They're great!" Right on cue, Bill broke into our new song, "Take a look at me." J. Michael and I fell into place doing the female do-wop backup, complete with misplaced dance steps (that would be me). The guy down at Hertz rentals was holding a phone in the air so someone at the other end could catch the show.

After our one-song performance––with two encores, followed by autograph signing--we had our car for a song. We then asked Annette if she could be our chauffeur and handle our bail money for the next week.

"Oh, my God, yes!" she cried. But Mr. Manager nixed that idea. He said the company didn't furnish drivers with their cars. But he *would* give us complete car insurance coverage at no charge. I pointed out to Mr. Manager how wise that car insurance coverage would be, knowing how musicians can be mischievous with their rental cars. You know, like car meets swimming pool, or a game of parking lot bumper cars or, my favorite—"Let's park the car in our room on the thirteenth floor of the Hilton!" Yes, insurance would be very good indeed.

Man, oh man, our whole Nashville trip was like some sort of magic herb while it lasted. We took up residence in a magnificent 150-year-old log cabin. Our digs were located behind a storybook Southern mansion complete with giant porch pillars. Johnny Cash Jr.'s drummer owned this place. We all hit it off quite well. As luck would have it, our new friend and landlord had a girlfriend who worked for the Country Music Award show. After meeting her and all the other lovelies in the office, it was clear that we were becoming the most famous unknown band in Nashville.

There was the day we were in the parking lot outside Fireside Recording studios where Bill met this girl who, with a single phone call, scheduled Bill to do a show the next night at the Blue Bird, a very coveted gig indeed. Bill played solo that night and rocked the Blue Bird to its foundation. J. Michael and I kept the girls at bay while running up a $350 bar tab. Old Jim Beam was very sneaky that evening. I never did hear who picked up the tab.

That same night we got ourselves invited to bluegrass legend Bill Monroe's eightieth birthday bash that was being held the next night at a club called The Bell Cove. When we showed up at the party, PBS had just started filming the event. Bill Monroe and his friends took the stage and played all night. The party at our table grew and grew and was fairly rowdy. Yea! We took over about eight tables and it seemed like every Southern beauty who was there that night wanted to spend time at our table. Whenever one of these beauties introduced herself to us, it was followed with "I'm part of Bill's (Monroe) stable, but he lets us do whatever we want or you want." Holy moley!

Now you're probably thinking , "Aha! Here are three boys who went totally, absolutely bad. They're probably worse than that guy who played in "Bad Santa" or those guys in the movie "Rock Star!"

Not a chance! I talked by phone to my bride Sioux twice a day. I filled her in on everything that had transpired between calls, I think. Anyway, the nurse has always made it clear that if I stray, she has a loaded enema bag with my name on it, and she knows how to use it.

We had such a good run on Music Row that we had to add dates to our tour, which meant we needed our rental car for a few more days. When we showed up back at Budget, there was a different crew on duty, and the "A Car for a Song" sign was gone. But when the new girl, whose name tag said "Lisa," brought us up on her computer, she said "You guys have a comp car, so there's no charge for adding dates. In fact, I'm giving you an upgrade. I heard all about you guys. I wish I'd been here."

"Thanks for the upgrade, Lisa," said J. Michael. "Ahh—we seem to have accumulated so much debris in the car it's almost impossible for us to get in and out. Also there's a strange pungent stench permeating the car, and we don't seem to be able to locate the source."

Lisa said, "Don't worry, we'll take care of everything. Could I have your autographs?" Since that trip, Budget's been my car rental place of choice.

That's something I really like—having a choice. A choice of what I drive, a choice of where I live, and a choice of what music I listen to. So why is food labeling exempt from having to list some of the ingredients that would influence my "to-use-or-not-to-use" choice? Like why not label "GM" products? No, no, I'm not talking about the auto-credit card company, but "Genetically Modified" food products. If GM foods are such a great idea, why do the manufacturers want to avoid labeling them? I want to know what I'm consuming. I realize there are a lot of folks who couldn't care less what kinds of food they ingest. That's cool. That's their choice.

Well, I'm stuck in the olden days. I prefer real food, not fake stuff that prior to 1973 would have had to be labeled as imitation foods. Now you're thinking, "Oh, he's a food snob." Not exactly! Miracle Whip is one of the food groups in my vocabulary—it's my choice. But adding herbicides to the corn gene pool just doesn't sound appetizing to me. I already have enough unnatural chemicals in my system, and the vast majority of them were not consumed for pleasure. Of all places in the world, you'd think that in the land of the free, we'd be free to choose GM or not!

Something Smells Fishy or Lizard Tails

As autumn starts to fade toward winter, I get a nice warm feeling inside knowing that I have picked the last of our Arkansas Black, Winesap, Sheep Nose, and other late apples from our heritage apple orchard. For my taste buds, you can't beat the flavor of a perfectly ripe Spitzenburg, King David, or Winter Banana. Once you've bitten into one of these great apples, you'll never again be able to eat those bland, cardboard, wax-covered things that pass in the grocery store for apples.

I'll bet there are still some folks out there who remember the almost daily use of the mighty apple. People once grew apples for frying, butter, cider (hard and sweet), drying, and pickling. In fact, I believe the apple has more culinary uses than any other fruit. I would love to hear from folks who remember how this great fruit was meant to be used.

With our larder filled, I thought life was perfect here at the old homestead—or almost. Sioux had finished up the last feeding of the year for our rose garden. Fish emulsion was her fertilizer of choice for the job. She set the gallon jug of fish emulsion on the bench by our kitchen door.

I had started in on the evening chores. Yes, I love sitting on our front porch sipping Jim Beam while partaking of other goodies as the day comes to a close. Utah was scratching at the door for me to let him out. Being lost in a fog of thoughts about nothing, I was a little slow at opening the door for him. When he bolted past me, I thought he must really have a full bladder, or he had gotten a whiff of one of the many tailless lizards he chases at every opportunity.

I'm quite sure Utah has a stash of lizard tails buried somewhere on our property. A few million years from now paleontologists will be writing about their great find: Utah's burial site containing the bones of hundreds and hundreds of lizard tails, but strangely, no lizard skeletons to be found anywhere. This will be cause for great debate within the academic community. Who were these ancient people who used this place as a holy site offering lizard tails to their god or gods? Did these tails come from virgin female lizards? Did people feed elsewhere on the lizard's body after the holy offering? With the use of carbon dating or something more precise, science will find that this site was used for a very short time. What happened to these people? Should I happen to find Utah's cache of lizard tails, I might bury a jar with a note explaining everything. But then again, why bother—those great debates will be rather interesting.

When I entered our living room, I froze like Bambi in the headlights of a runaway eighteen-wheeler.

"Good God!" I said. "What is that stench?" The smell sucked the breath right out of me, just as if a plastic bag from the dry cleaners had been zip-locked over my head.

"So this is what it smells like in a fish-processing plant," I thought. I have smelled strong tuna before, but it never made my eyes water or my lips feel like they were being pricked by a thousand razor-sharp pins. Maybe I was passing out. But I wasn't so lucky. I wiped the tears from my eyes and focused on numerous nasty-looking black splotches on our fairly new carpet. I ran to the kitchen for some very absorbent paper towels and hollered to Sioux, who was outside the kitchen door, "Come quick! Utah is very sick!"

"He should be," she informed me tartly. Turns out he had knocked the fish emulsion, which had an unsecured cap, from the bench onto the ground. There he slurped up the vile-smelling stuff as his ancient ancestors would have done. Feed. Regurgitate. Feed some more. I'll bet his ancestors didn't have a nice carpet to throw up on, though.

I went to work cleaning the carpet, longing for those nose plugs I wore as a kid while swimming at the YMCA. I held my breath, and when I thought my lungs would burst, I ran outside gulping in the cool fresh air. Nurse Sioux went to work checking out Utah. Eyes were fine, gums had good color. Oh, but his breath! She got out the Tom's toothpaste and a little Scope and brushed his teeth. Man, he hated this whole process. He wasn't buying the fact that he wasn't getting near us with his leach-field breath. He thought he had trained us better.

After a very long while, I got the stains out of the rug, but not the smell. I told Sioux that if professional cleaners couldn't get it out, I was taking the carpet and pad to the dump. After several more attempts to remove the smell, we did call in the pros. They tried working their magic on it. No luck. Finally, they supplied me with some sort of super fume remover that took more than a month, but our carpet is finally back to its old self.

Just like our carpet, politics will take more than one or two scrubbings to clean it up—lobbyists and special interest groups are deeply imbedded. We'll have to scrub long and hard, but I think the cleansing is worth our effort.

No More Excuses or French Kissing

Do you ever wonder why you don't do the outdoor activities you once loved in the past? "Like what activities?" you might ask. Well, like fishing, biking, hiking, birding, arrowhead hunting, river-running, road-tripping—anything that got you out-of-doors and away from home. Me, I love to go camping. Never mattered if it was an overnighter or a month-long outing. Now, I find I rarely go camping, but that's going to change this year.

Sioux and I, Tuesday, Utah, and Chloe the cat will make several pilgrimages into the wilderness this year. No more excuses like "Who will water, weed, and deadhead the garden?" No excuses due to my ingrown toenail, ingrown hairs, or hemorrhoids. Even jamming, canning, dehydrating, or running out of Jim Beam will not do as an excuse. I've entered the "no-more-excuses" era. Fortunately, I've never used the lamest of all excuses, "I'll miss my favorite TV show." If you hear yourself coming up with that one, then immediately chain your TV to the back of your car and drag it for a few miles until it is dead.

One of my favorite camping excursions was to Hidden Lake in the Sierra La Sal Mountains of southeast Utah. It was there that Ricky Lee Costanza, Ken Hoffman, Doo Doo the Wonder Dog, and I constructed, without permits, a magnificent lean-to, sheltering us from the weather and the elements, but mostly from ourselves. Camp was tucked away in a grove of old-growth aspen trees, surrounded by a fifty-foot barrier of "wind-thrown" fallen aspen. You had to be steady and balanced (not mentally though) as you transversed this slick high-wire tree puzzle or you'd take a header.

So, I took a header. I hit hard, with a faint whimpering scream.

My newly found soprano voice was not because of a fractured bone or being impaled on a stiff, jagged, mangling piece of wood. *No,* it was from the sound of breaking glass followed by a scent that permeated the air with a mouth-watering sour-mash aroma. Inside my pack, my underwear, socks, and toothbrush received an eighty percent proof sterilization. I had broken a bottle of liquid refreshment. This tragic news was met at camp with a deep guttural and agonizing wail that sounded like an Italian wake for a recently departed brother. Once the sniveling stopped, Ricky Lee and Ken produced liquid refreshments of their own from *their* packs. Those two were always prepared.

"Prepared"--a word that makes me think about the time Ricky Lee and Ken took me on my first mule deer hunt. I had been in Utah only a few days, direct from Avon, Indiana. I had never seen a deer other than a black velvet painting of Bambi. I didn't even know people still hunted them. Those two outlaws were always prepared and worked together like a well-oiled drill rig. I would never have guessed you could hunt "mulies" from the window of a Datsun 510 during a full moon with a single shot twenty-two rifle in Arches National Monument, now a park. Well, you did back then!

I felt like "Grasshopper" from the old *Kung-Fu* TV show, as these two learned teachers took me under their co-joined wings to teach me the old ways of the locals. This Grasshopper learned fast. Line your car trunk with plastic, have a razor-sharp knife or two, and if you need more than one shot, then you shouldn't own a firearm. Ricky Lee emphasized to Grasshopper the importance of leaving a fresh steamy gut pile by the side of the road. When I asked the wise one why, he said, "Food for the park rangers—they aren't paid much. And then there's the coyote, always a friend. The pile also feeds the foxes, skunks, vultures, ravens, magpies, hornets, blowflies, and tourists. Especially tourists, as they've been known to perish along these roadways." Ken chimed in on Ricky Lee's speech, "We eat, everyone eats."

Now don't get your underwear all knotted up and put yourself into a tizzy over this event. It happened a long time ago. I did learn from those two outlaw teachers—later, of course, that if you paid a tax to the king in October, you would be granted permission to hunt "mulies" on the king's land for two weeks, as long as you carried the king's paper bearing his official seal.

Back in those days there were a number of the king's laws that were hard to enforce in southeast Utah. Civilization hadn't yet destroyed this part of the world. Bars were in abundance, like Frank's Place, 66 Club, Wagon Wheel, T&C, Alibi, Silver Dollar, Woody's, and the Lrae, where Earl would sell you illegal shots of some bathtub concoction that was sure to make you go blind. Southeast Utah was filled with uranium miners (worst of the lot), prospectors, roughnecks, cowboys, sheepherders, Navajos, Utes, beautiful women, The Holiday Gang, dead cars, dead trucks, dead dreams, and graveyards. By God, it was heaven. All gone now except Woody's, and it's been civilized.

Now that I've gotten completely off track, let's get back to camping. On this particular day in history, we had all caught the king's legal limit of rainbow trout. As the sun set, the sky turned from turquoise blue to flaming yellow to a dark volcanic red-orange. What a magnificent sight. We filled our bellies with fried trout, onions, and buttered spuds, chased with good cheer and war stories. The good smoke still filled the air as we crawled into the lean-to and our sleeping bags.

I woke up shivering. My ten-dollar GovCo sleeping bag, with its good-to-sixty-degrees rating, according to its tag, was way into its failure zone. It was barely above freezing. I couldn't move my feet, as Doo Doo had wormed his way to the bottom of my bag to stay warm. Ken was way too close to me for comfort, as he was snoring in my ear, and he was known for dreams about that dreaded life in the "big house"--also known as prison. I rolled over on my side, about to plant an elbow in his parched, whistling lips, when I froze. Not six feet away from me, standing on Ricky Lee's chest, was a rather large skunk, or, as we called them, a "Pepe LePew." Pepe was nose to nose with Ricky Lee, whose eyes were bigger than baby moon hubcaps. I didn't know anyone's eyes could expand to such an enormous size. I had to fight my instinct to run off into the night screaming "Skunk!"

Ken stirred from his dream about prison life, as I whispered, ever so softly through gritted teeth, "Don't move, prison boy. Skunk!" He could see I was looking in Ricky Lee's direction. Ever so slowly Ken turned his head toward Ricky Lee and witnessed old Pepe licking Ricky Lee's lips. I was amazed at Ricky Lee's poise. Was this a rabid skunk that had fallen in love with our friend? If it were not rabid, it soon would be after French-kissing Ricky Lee. It seemed like an eternity that these two stared into each other's longing eyes. Would there be love, or a torrent of rancid perfume from Pepe? I guessed he finally decided on "no action here" as he turned and walked down the length of Ricky Lee's body. Then, with one last look back, he scurried off into the night.

Except for me, everyone was out of his sleeping bag faster than a quick Ex-Lax reaction. The zipper on my ten-dollar sleeping bag had jammed. I crawled out of the lean-to, dragging my bag around my waist with Doo Doo, who hadn't stirred, still in the bottom trying to keep warm.

We were all talking rapidly about the events straight out of a B-movie in which we had just starred. Ken was breathing life back into our all but dead fire when a scream pierced the night with such intensity that we fell silent. "Mountain lion!" That chilling scream is forever etched into my last remaining brain cell.

Yep, I'm ready to hit the camping campaign trail again. Chowing down under the stars, freezing in the cold weather, campfire smoke, mosquitoes, ticks, snakes, storytelling, and living new stories. My newer and prettier sidekicks--my bride, Sioux, dogs Tuesday and Utah, and our niece Chloe the cat--will be in for a new adventure, too. What if Pepe tries to French-kiss Tuesday or Utah? After all, they're black and white and could be related. Sioux actually suggested that our present life is like "camping out," and we could have the next big adventure in the back of our own orchard. Heck, we have skunks, ticks, mosquitoes, mountain lions, a sky full of stars, the rapid-flowing creek, and enough room for a big roaring fire, too. All we need is a four-poster bed with a down comforter.

No more excuses. I'm going camping. How 'bout you?

The Utah Outlaws on the sand flats outside Moab, Utah (bottom row: JD, Al "El Supremo" McLeod, J. Michael Pearce and Ricky Lee Costanza; back row: Chris "Mad Man" Allen, 1998

Running on Fear

I was soaked in sweat as I woke from a restless sleep filled with flying-creature nightmares. My chest was tight and it ached. Was my left arm numb? Sioux was sleeping soundly, but the dogs were wide awake. Utah was lying on my feet looking at me with his head cocked to the left and his ears perked up. I must have been moaning or groaning or making some sort of unspeakable noise. Little Ms. Tuesday was staring at me with a concerned look on her face. She decided that the cleaning of my ears might be in order. Tuesday's ear-cleaning brought me out of my chemical fog, and I realized I wasn't having a heart attack—it was just the day I had to deal with that incompetent industry known as "The Airlines."

What other industry could run at ninety percent capacity, pay its CEOs tens of millions of dollars in bonuses and compensation, go bankrupt, then show up on Capitol Hill in DC in their super-stretch limos to perform a lap dance for their politician cronies, who then expunge them from their contract obligations to their employees? This is called "the free marketplace." I may have gone to an unaccredited high school in Avon, Indiana, but even there this particular "free marketplace" would have been referred to by its true names—"Welfare," "Let's put it to the working stiff," or "We're the king; you're the peasant."

I'm flying to the state that was the twenty-eighth to join the Union, but had only enough material and thread to sew one star on their state flag. You guessed it, I'm going to Texas. Boerne, Texas, to be exact. Sioux dropped me off at the Medford Airport at 7:50 a.m. for a 9:20 flight to Portland, then Dallas, and on to San Antonio.

My 9:20 flight was cancelled.

The plane was sent back to Portland due to "low clouds." Nobody in the loading chute (as I call it) could believe the "low clouds" story, as we could see the hills of east Medford. Everyone scrambled back to the ticket counter for re-ticketing, or a hitchhiking adventure, or the worst case scenario: a ride on a Greyhound bus. I rescheduled for the next flight out, whatever time that would be. Of course, I had now missed all connecting flights. I wandered around our two-gate "international airport," and in one minute I had seen it all, so I decided to check through security to the loading chute for the second time that day.

I removed my shoes yet again and gave thanks that the shoe bomber from London had used his shoes for his pea-brained failed terrorist attack. What if he had used his jock strap to hide explosives? Holy moley, could you imagine the hassle of passing security then?

So I was feeling blessed as I walked through the metal detector in my matching socks. But what was that beep? I was ordered by the TSA officer, "Sir, empty your pockets, remove your belt, and try again." I told him that I just came through here thirty minutes ago and all had been fine. There was nothing in my pockets, and my belt buckle was made of pewter. It *never* sets off the security alarm system.

"Sir, remove your belt."

Off with the belt and through the metal detector again. There was that beeping sound. So I was escorted to the little glass room where everyone who passed by could watch my interrogation. I wondered if this cubicle was set up to contain my body parts and those of the TSA officer should I detonate myself for all to see.

The hand-held metal detector indicated that there was something in my shirt pocket. I felt around and found three or four micro paper clips that had passed through security earlier. Another wave of the wand and it still beeped. It took three passes before I had all the micro paper clips out of my pocket. I had no idea where they had come from, but there they were. After being frisked (which made me laugh because I am ticklish), I was told that I could now pass on through to the loading chute.

I walked over to the x-ray scanner to pick up my carry-on bag. The TSA lady was holding up my toothpaste, and she had a very stern look stamped on her pasty, lumpy, unfriendly face.

"Is this yours, sir?"

I should have just said "no" and abandoned my boxer shorts, floss, and toothbrush, but she knew it was mine.

"Yes, ma'am, that's my Tom's Fluoride-Free toothpaste." Then it occurred to me that fluoride-free might be illegal now. Before I could assure her that I would never brush my teeth again, I was asked if I were aware of the new law passed a few months ago banning all liquid containers over three ounces from being carried onto a flight from the outside world. I informed Ms. TSA that, as is the case with most laws that are passed in this country, no one had stopped by my house to inform me. I also pointed out that thirty minutes earlier everything in my carry-on bag had passed this same security screening station and was hunky dory. Maybe, just maybe, that was because the label said "toothpaste" and not "tooth liquid?" Paste is not a liquid. Right?

At that point I could see her pudgy jaw muscle twitching as she brought all 5'3," 235 pounds of herself up to an authoritative position and asked me if I was arguing with her. The look from the deep inner part of her dilated pupils told me to say, "No, ma'am!" I could see it right then; I was on the verge of being tasered with 50,000 volts and Ms. TSA would then pin me to the ground, while using a can of mace on each eye and screaming, "You want to argue with me now, Mister Smarty Panties? You are going to Guantanomo Bay, Cuba. Smoke that, why don't you!"

I did ask for a receipt for my confiscated property, but was denied.

This was just the beginning of an air travel trip that would take years of therapy to reverse my newfound fear of toothpaste. Every time I look at a tube of toothpaste I see Ms. TSA, Freddy Krueger, internment camps, Terrorist Alert Orange, cameras at every intersection, freedoms given up without question—a country fueled by fear, running on fear. Fear will do us in faster than any terrorist ever could, and I'm fearful of *that*!

Older than Dirt or Crap from China

The other day, I was having a phone conversation with one of my Utah outlaw sidekicks, punk rocker Ricky Lee Costanza. He said, "Do you remember the old fishing hole that Chris 'Madman' Allen, you and I used to frequent on Beaver Lake in the La Sal Mountains?"

"You bet I do. That was the place where you showed me your favorite fishing lure, the Dupont spinner. With that lure, you could fill your limit and then some in one or two casts. Man, I'll always remember Beaver Lake! The place where I offered up so many brain cells to the god of 'may your stringer be overfilled with trout.' Where I spent so much time face down, with unblinking slits for eyes, and a permanent super-glued smile in place. Oh yeah, I remember that fishing hole."

Ricky Lee said, "Well, brace yourself." I thought, "Oh, my God, they've built time-share condos with an eighteen-hole Tiger Woods pro golf course or a Radon Ray shopping center complete with a Wallymart. Or worse, a rehab center for wayward local fishermen." He proceeded to tell me that it was no longer a lake, but a pretty meadow, and not a fishing hole to be found.

"Holy Moley, Rick, do you realize that makes you older than dirt?" (I excluded myself, of course.) "How many folks do you know who have lived long enough to see their favorite fishing hole—no, the whole lake—transformed into a meadow? By God, man, that's plum scary!"

Ricky Lee said, "Well, maybe it never really existed. I mean, with the state of mind we were all in in those days." I pondered that point, but I knew it had existed, because I would pull trout out of my used Ward's freezer in December. While eating that succulent trout jaw muscle meat, I would dream about our fishing camp at Beaver Lake. About that time the motor mansion in which Rickey Lee was traveling passed into a dead cell phone zone. We lost our connection.

I guess I've been around long enough now to have seen a lot of changes take place around me. There are our two Border Collies: Tuesday doesn't play ball nonstop twenty-four hours a day anymore—it's a much more manageable eighteen-hour day. Utah has to take a nap on our gravel driveway in the summer sun between each of his chicken round-ups—in and out of the coop a dozen times a day, checking on the girls. I get exhausted just watching him. Our two Australian Shepherds, Boogie and Bentley, have come, lived the good life, and gone. They now live through the tree peonies that my bride, Sioux, and I planted over them. Then there is Doo Doo the Wonder Dog, who is planted in Los Angeles. He is in an area that I'm sure will be classified as an EPA toxic clean-up site one day. Why? No dog ever had worse foul breath--or more personality.

Gone, too, is that proud bumper sticker "Made in America." It has been replaced with the ubiquitous "Made in China." A logo for a Communist country, that when I was a kid we were told was an evil doer! Now we are told that China is our friend, so it is okay for them to ship us poison ingredients that get used in our dog food and fed to farm-raised trout and salmon (which, for my palate, were already inedible).

Then there are the recalls on children's toys for lead paint (now you know where all the lead paint went when it was banned in America years ago) and flammable materials. Do you think this stuff just got lost in translation somehow? In fact, 100% of toy recalls so far this year have been "crap from China." That has a nice ring to it: "Crap From China." It is definitely more descriptive than "Made in China," don't you think?

Don't get me wrong. I know we in this country are not perfect in our relations with the environment. Recently we had a bunch of onion growers right here in eastern Oregon who illegally applied the carbon furan pesticide Furadan to control the thrips that were damaging the onions.

The upside is that those onions never made it to market. The Oregon Department of Agriculture saw to that. Unlike the Chinese shrimp, catfish, eel, basa, and dace that are now found to be laced with drug residues. How about that toothpaste and cold medicine contaminated with diethylene glycol? In Panama, there were 100 people, mostly kids, confirmed to have died from it. Authorities speculate that there were hundreds more deaths. Don't you just love "Crap from China"?

China is serious about tackling its tainted food safety problem (you bet, can you say "Avian flu?") They executed Zheng Xiaoyu, the former director of China's Food and Drug Agency. I wonder if he was the former director before or after the execution. He traded his okay on hundreds of medicines for a pocketful of cheap Chinese cash. Those meds were never tested and didn't do what the manufacturer said they would. Am I impressed with the execution of Zheng Xiaoyu? Heavens, no. Gangsters always liquidate their people when there is a problem that needs correcting.

We, the consumers, are really the ones to blame. We control the purse strings, but we seem to salivate all over ourselves at the opportunity to buy cheap "Crap from China." Well, I've had enough. Just say no to "Crap from China." That is our new household policy. Yes, I cleared it with my bride first. The dogs are on board, too—they're still ticked about the toxic dog food.

I would think if one believed in global warming, one would not want to send one more dollar to China, the land of few environmental regulations and even less enforcement. Did you know that in less than a year China will surpass America in CO_2 emissions and will rapidly leave us in a cloud of smoke?

With all of the unaccountable outsourcing, imports, and a war that is sinking us ever deeper in debt, do you think that China will offer to bail us out? I feel like we are falling into a bottomless black pit filled with vipers, with no net below to catch US. I see no leadership with a vision, and none on the horizon, to show us the way out of this dismal trade relationship. That scares me a lot more than Beaver Lake evolving into a meadow.

Deep-Fried Twinkie Coma or Flashing Cherries

On my recent visit to Texas, my big (he's taller) brother Jeff was showing me the sights of the hill country while driving on Texas back roads. We traveled through Boerne, Welfare, Waring, and up to Kerrville, Texas. Our outing took us past some magnificent oak trees and fabulous old stone buildings, mostly built by legal German immigrants who had settled the area in the 1800s. We followed the Guadalupe River, which was running crystal clear with majestic cypress trees lining her banks. This made for a nice backdrop as we reminisced about tales from our youth. But I told Jeff that, as nice as the countryside looked, it didn't hold water compared to southwestern Oregon.

However, when we arrived in Kerrville, I was feeling quite poorly—a queasy stomach (too many deep-fried Twinkies) and lightheaded (not enough Jim Beam). I just felt like an old cow pie, so we decided to head back to the barn. The quickest way home was south and down I-10. I was drifting in and out of the dream world in an upright fetal position when Jeff pointed out that a state trooper who had been heading north was now dropping down to the median strip and heading south, and moving like a rocket that had locked in on us.

I told Jeff, "Don't worry, you're only running at seventy-six to seventy-eight miles per hour, which is very slow for this Hemi engine you have. Besides, we're following the flow of traffic here. Don't worry."

We pulled over, and the red lights followed us from the passing lane right on over to the emergency stopping lane. Not a good sign. The officer walked up to the driver's side and asked my brother for his driver's license and proof of insurance. Jeff gave the officer those legal documents and asked why he was being stopped. He was told, "You were speeding and following too close." The trooper then asked me if I had any identification. I gave him my official Oregon driver's license and was asked if all the information was current. "You bet," I said.

"So you are still living in Oregon?" he asked. I couldn't read his thoughts through his reflective sunglasses, and I was feeling like I might be about ready to leave yesterday's barbecued Ding-Dongs along the side of the road. My stomach was getting worse. (My brother had assured me that this particular dish was Texas haute cuisine.)

"That's right. My brother is just showing me some of your Texas countryside."

"You claim him for your brother?"

Hmmm, that doesn't sound good. So I said, "Uh-- usually." The trooper went back to his car with the flashing cherries on top to run a check on the Rogers brothers. As I rested my numb head on the window, we pondered the comment the trooper had made. I said, "Maybe he was just trying to lighten things up a bit before he gives you a ticket." God, I was feeling *worse* than a cow pie. I was swearing off deep-fried Ho-Hos as well. I needed to go lie down.

About that time, the trooper walked up on my side of the truck. I pushed the power button, and my window dropped down. The light breeze felt good on my face, as I noticed the trooper's right hand on the butt of his gun, holding my driver's license in his left hand. He asked, "Do you go by James or Jim?"

"Neither. My name is JD."

"Well, JD, there is a warrant for your arrest. Would you step out of the truck?" Now I was feeling really ill.

"There must be some sort of mistake, officer," I said as I climbed out of the truck. Maybe the TSA officer at the Medford airport had decided she'd teach me a good lesson for trying to board a plane with a six-ounce Tom's Toothpaste in my carry-on. No! Maybe it was the Mercedes that Chris "Madman" Allen and I rolled in Grand Junction, Colorado, while on a test drive back in 1977. No! Maybe it was that Oklahoma credit card (also known as gas siphoning) that I used to use. But I think the statute of limitations is up on all that stuff.

Then I was thinking maybe jail wouldn't be so bad. I was feeling like I might need a visit to an emergency room. If I were in custody, the state of Texas would have to pay for my hospital visit. On the other hand, I have seen way too many movies about prison life. I was a longhair in the South. Not good. In fact, this was feeling really, really, really bad.

The trooper asked me if there was anything I needed to tell him. Leaning heavily against the truck, I noticed an *Applegator* lying in the back seat and told the officer, "I'm the editor of our local paper, the *Applegator*." I was thinking homeland security might be ticked about something we had printed. The trooper mused, "Oregon. That's a blue state. You didn't go for George Bush in the last election, did you?"

"Who?" I responded. At that point, my brother walked around the truck, and the trooper ordered him to stay where he was, saying, "There's a warrant for your arrest, too." This was just getting more hunky-dory by the minute, but at least I would know someone at the Texas Big House.

Jeff said, "A warrant for what?" A DWU., he was told. Jeff asked, "What's a DWU?" The trooper said, "Driving While Ugly!" Then he started laughing, turned to shake my hand, and chortled, "You've been had, JD."

Turns out these tough hombres, my brother and the trooper, are good friends. Now, that's a good joke—once you start breathing normally again, change your pants, and drop the name Bubba from your vocabulary. Whew!

While I had been nodding in and out of my deep-fried Twinkie coma, Jeff knew his trooper buddy was working I-10 and called him on his cell phone. And they had set the whole thing up for the end of his shift.

Jeff got me as good as I've been got. The bar has been raised. So I'm now looking for a new best friend in the FBI or CIA to knock on Jeff's door and inform him that they need to do some serious orifice probing.

I revert to the late 1960's and sported a cape once again, 2003.

Late Night Parties with Groupies or Are We Reading Lips Here?

I used to have this motto: "If my music is too loud, you're too old." That was before Hip Hop and Rap. Turn it OFF! Well, most of it. Does this mean I'M too old? I refuse to answer that on the grounds that it might incriminate me. Thank God for the Fifth Amendment. Actually, it doesn't really matter much. I can't hear for crap anymore.

You're thinking, "Ha ha, your loud music blew out your eardrums." That may be true for some rockers, but not in my case. Excuse me for a minute while I put on some music by Buck Cherry, Jett, Billy Idol and AC/DC. There—that sets the mood for writing about my hearing loss.

A few years back, my bride, Sioux, and I were at the Oregon State Fair up in Salem (I love the chicken exhibits). We were wandering aimlessly (or I was) after much wine tasting, when we came across a booth that was offering free hearing testing. We discussed whether to have our hearing tested (Sioux's choice), or do more wine tasting (my choice).

So we had our hearing tested. "Ride on" was my response to the technician who performed my test, when he told me my hearing was excellent. He couldn't believe I ever played in rock and roll bands. "Yep," I said, "It's great to know all those years of Marshall amps blasting thousands of watts of guitar notes didn't destroy my hearing."

I couldn't wait to call my folks and tell them. "Ya, baby, my loud music didn't blast my hearing to bits." My mom was sure I would be deaf by my mid-twenties. I had survived another chapter from my previous life as "the unknown rock star." It was time for more wine tasting.

A few years after that I found myself saying, "Huh?" "What?" and giving the wrong answers to a lot of questions. That is something you don't want to do when law enforcement wishes to have a few words with you. It's a real bummer when they say, "Mr. Rogers, maybe you'd like to change your answer to my question," and, of course, I still answer with "Huh?"

Our phone would ring, and I wouldn't hear it if I was in another room. This got to be so pathetic that our Border Collie, Tuesday, started barking at me when the phone rang.

Then she'd herd me to whichever room the portable phone had been misplaced. What the heck was going on here?

Prior to my hearing loss, I had a run of some health issues where I ingested several different types of antibiotics over a course of time. No, this was not for something I had picked up from those late night parties with groupies in years past. Unfortunately for me, a side effect of some antibiotics can be hearing loss. That's much more serious than a broken guitar string.

I now wear hearing aids. Of course, when folks find out they say, "Too much loud music I bet." You lose the bet—it was from antibiotics. I should have said no to drugs, because it is a drag to have your hearing short-circuit on you. I am a long way from deaf, but even with hearing aids, soft voices are very difficult to understand.

Movie night with friends has improved. I no longer have to ask, "Are we reading lips here?" They would then turn the television sound up and promptly install earplugs.

I put off getting my hearing aids for quite a while. I couldn't picture myself walking around with a mountain sheep horn protruding from each ear. I just didn't think that would set the fashion world on fire. It was hard for me to imagine a fashion show where the announcer would say, "And now we have a full curl mountain sheep horn in each ear, smartly attached with Crazy Glue for that ever perfect permanent look. These hearing horns come in three marvelous colors: chartreuse green, hottie pink, and ravish me red." I don't think so.

Luckily you can get hearing aids today that you can barely see, or, in my case, not at all. Love that long hair. My hearing aids are programmed via computer. So if I need an adjustment, wha-la, it's done in no time at all. I can hear the phone ring from different rooms now, but little Miss Tuesday still barks at me and herds me to the phone, along with anybody else she thinks should answer that annoying ringing thing.

Speaking of annoying, one advantage to hearing aids is that I can turn them off whenever Free Traders open their mouths. I don't have to listen to how great it is that we import more cars from Mexico than we export to the rest of the world. There was a time when we produced forty percent of the world's manufactured goods. Now we're selling off our infrastructure to foreign corporations. We've gone from the most self-sufficient nation in history, where our industrial workers were the best paid in the universe, to deficits, bankruptcies, lost pensions and health care, and at least a generation's worth of financial liabilities. Yes, siree, the one-party system has served us well!

When I have my hearing aids turned on, even though the sound isn't perfect, it sure beats the alternative, right officer? So if this unknown rock star (is there any type of person more vain?) can wear hearing aids, then anybody can.

Miscommunication or The Lark Rocket

Why is it so difficult for people to communicate with each other? I sure have had my share of "Communication Breakdown," a great Led Zeppelin song. For me, the breakdown usually happens when I assume or misinterpret what was being said in the first place. Just ask my bride, Sioux. She'll come to me with a problem, be it gardening, people, or work-related. Right off the bat, I want to fix the problem--a Mars thing. Whereas she usually just wants me to say, "Everything will be all right"--a Venus thing. You'd think after twenty years of marriage, by now I'd know the correct answer. But noooooooooo! I guess I'm a slow learner, with a talent for misinterpretation of the female gender. I've been told that you're supposed to "read between the lines," or, in my case, look between the pictures. But wouldn't it just be easier if everyone just said what it was that they really wanted? If you say, "I want chocolate raspberry ice cream," your want is very clear. Versus, "Oh, I don't know, whatever." That leaves a lot of room for misinterpretation.

Our two Border Collies, Tuesday and Utah, are very clear in their communications with me. Maybe that is because they have trained me better than Sioux has trained me. For instance, when I'm eating a bowl of Cookies & Cream ice cream, their pathetic stares and whimpers are very clear. They are communicating to me that "we are half starved to death, and we are very deserving of our own bowl of ice cream. In fact, you owe us many bowls of ice cream with all of the homeland security tasks we perform here at the fort, and the chicken herding we do for you."

Speaking of chicken herding, the other day our neighbor, Linda Fischer, pulled into our driveway with old Utah in her back seat. Seems that Utah had been patrolling our orchard deer fence when he came to a place where Mr. Bear had decided to flex his muscles. Mr. Bear had bent a fence post almost to the ground. He wandered around the orchard leaving mysterious piles and helping himself to the windfall apples that I hadn't yet picked up. Fortunately, I had already picked all the apples from the trees, and thus avoided the maiming and mangling of my apple tree branches. From the twenty feet of fence that Mr. Bear had conveniently laid on the ground, Utah could see the Fischer's free-ranging chickens. So, with no obstacles, and being a Border Collie, he decided that those wayward chickens needed to be rounded up and put to bed, even though it was only noon.

Utah was communicating, "I need more work." So I'm going to fix him up with a sign that reads, "Will work for dog cookies" or "Hey, mister, can you spare a biscuit?" This action makes perfect economic sense, since either one would offset the expenditure for dog cookies (bribes) we experience here at the ranch.

Years ago, good friend Boyd Uselton and I decided that we would put a new rock band together, one of many band experiences we shared. We had met a guitar player at Sack's Brother's pawnshop in downtown Indianapolis, Indiana. This was the place where Boyd and I used to hang out for hours lusting over the many Gibson Les Paul guitars that decorated the wall, or ooohing and aaahing over the beautiful tuck and rolled Kustom amps displayed on the floor. Boyd and I were communicating our wants and desires for these sweet, beautiful, "I would never cheat on you" instruments.

In those visual mind-melting days, Boyd drove the most hip automobile in all of Avon, Indiana. In the right frame of mind, you could marvel over the fine lines of his 1962 Studebaker Lark. It shone with a hot pink hood, roof, and trunk, with yummy watermelon and lime-green fenders, all covered in an icing of psychedelic stick-on flowers representing every color in the rainbow—a love bucket on wheels. When cruising in the Lark rocket, we always received a notorious amount of road rage, flashing red lights, and memorable sign language.

We decided to go to audition our new pawnshop buddy's guitar skills and his gear. Using a map that he had scribbled on the back of a used pawn card, we piloted the Lark rocket deeply into the world of despair and addiction, where the air hung heavy with the stench of rot and decay, a landscape that resembled a nuke test site, but without the warm glow. We had ventured into the Indianapolis ghetto. Around ten p.m., after a disastrous "audition," Boyd and I communicated that we would pass on this particular guitar player, who had only four strings and no amp.

On our way home, we were sitting at a red light on Massachusetts Avenue, when Boyd pointed out a bookstore that was still open. He wanted to go in and see if they had a book on the occult that he had been looking for. I pointed out that this was not the neighborhood to be doing late-night book shopping.

"Haven't you noticed the boarded-up storefronts, the sidewalks littered with broken wine bottles and God knows what else? What do you think the girls we just passed were doing? It's a little cool out for such skimpy evening wear, don't you think?"

Boyd said, "We'll be okay. I'll park in front of that big old church, just down that side street there." I obviously wasn't communicating. We turned off Massachusetts Avenue, drove about a block down a very dimly lit side street and parked in front of the church. I pointed out to Boyd how very deserted-looking this area was and asked him if he noticed the broken windows in the church. Boyd said, "Rogers, you can wait in the car if you want."

"Are you kidding me? I'm not staying in this car. And by the way, don't you find it odd that you think we'll be safe parked in front of this church while you search for some book on the occult?"

Boyd just smiled and said, "Let's go." Maybe if I had peed my pants I would have better communicated my uneasiness. I did pray that our musical instruments would be safe in the trunk. Of course, they didn't have the occult book that Boyd was looking for, but he was stoked anyway because he bought a *Playboy,* and it was a coup for him because he was underage.

As we walked back to the car, a cold breeze blew some paper litter up from among the Boone's Farm wine bottles that covered the sidewalk. I should have known that this was a sign from above, and not a good one, either. We were almost to the car, when a group of six or seven guys hollered at us from the front steps of the church. I don't know what it was they said, but the tone communicated a sickening feeling to me. We continued at a normal walk, not quite a run. Running prey is what a pack of predators is looking for, right? There was now an old rusted Chevy beater parked in front of the Lark rocket--a new development.

We leaped into the Lark. But why weren't we moving yet? Come on, Boyd! Get this puppy going! He said, "I can't get the key in the ignition." Good God. I'd seen this same scene in many movies, and it always ended badly. At this point, we were communicating panic to each other.

"Got a square?" came a voice from a head that was part way into the car window on my side of the car. That's right, my window was rolled up only two-thirds of the way. It was broken. I didn't have a clue as to what this future "liferboy" for the Indiana state penal system was asking me. So I responded, "Oh, no. We're not square."

"Hey, dumb ****,--gotta square or not?"

I was thinking, "Come on, Boyd, start this piece of crap!"

"Who's a square?" I said.

At that moment, Boyd's key entered the ignition, and the mighty rocket's four cylinders fired to life. Boyd was grinding gears, as he tried to get the three speeds on the column into reverse. Liferboy thrust his arm through the broken car window with what looked to me like a machete. At the same time, Boyd found reverse and dumped the clutch. The Lark lunged backwards, throwing me forward into the car dash. Fortunately for me, that made Liferboy's knife miss its mark--he just slashed the back of my absolutely favorite shirt, drawing only a little bit of blood. I grabbed Liferboy's knife-wielding hand by his wrist with both of my hands. It took every bit of adrenalin strength I could muster to keep my hold on him, as the Lark rocket careened up and over the curb, across the church's dead lawn, and right into their empty stone announcement marque, with a hard thud. Boyd's defensive driving in reverse (Avon High's driver's ed class paid off) had sent Liferboy's gang tumbling to the pavement littered with broken glass and—I hoped--other jagged goodies. The gears were grinding again as Boyd searched for any gear that would get us moving forward and out of this bad movie. A hailstorm of chains and pipes rained down on the Lark as we blasted off the dead lawn and onto the street, followed by a pop-pop-pop that took out the right taillight. I was still holding Liferboy's wrist so tightly that I was surprised that the car window didn't break out. All he could do was scream at me in a profane verbal assault. I heard some new verbiage that I later added to my own language skills. Shared communication.

As the car's engine screamed in first gear, I could not hold onto Liferboy's wrist anymore. But before I was forced to release him, I opened my eyes for the first time since the storm of metal on metal pelted down upon us. With only a car window between us, I was looking right into Liferboy's eyes. His communication was: "I'm going to rip your butt out and choke you to death with it." Then, as I released him, his new expression communicated, "I'm screwed!" As his body met the pavement with a pleasing sound and we screeched away, Boyd said, "My God, Rogers, I thought you were dead!"

Here's something more I'd like to communicate: Our lives would surely be a lot easier if our elected officials could communicate truthfully with us--"We the People"—half as well as my two dogs communicate with me. Every four years we get to hear about the grandiose schemes that will come our way "if you only send me to the White House." You bet! Our corporate-sponsored one-party system has proven over and over that, after each election, promises boil down to a dessert plate without the cake.

Wouldn't it be novel if we were to hear some honest communication such as, "All lobbyists and spin doctors have been deported to Beijing"? Instead, we hear the typical deceitful, cunning communication that flows like a fetid, filthy, flash flood out of Washington DC: "We're here for you, open your wallets now." It's all a game of fool's gold, but who's the fool?

Twitching Or Praise the Lord

I had just finished watching the last DVD of the first season of HBO's "Deadwood" when I realized I was hooked on yet another soap opera. At that point our Border Collie, Tuesday, stood up on the foot of the bed and started gagging. "No, no, no, Tuesday, let's go outside. Come on, hurry." But she didn't listen to me. Women rarely do. She proceeded to regurgitate some god-awful, dreadful, smelly, watery substance that had me gagging and running to the bathroom. After I recovered, I stripped the bed before the mattress was tattooed with yet another stain.

Poor little Tuesday had more than a minor tummy ache. Her eyes were dilated; she held her head up so that her nose was pointing toward the ceiling; her nose was dry but runny, her body was cold to the touch, and she had developed a dreadful body twitch. Oh my God, help! My bride and private nurse, Sioux, was out of town. I was on my own.

I was afraid that since it was 11 p.m., our vet wouldn't be available. I was very relieved after I called her and she said, "Bring her in." All I needed now was a police escort with flashing red lights and screaming sirens for my midnight emergency room vet run. But with county budget cuts, I figured that wasn't going to happen.

I kept telling Tuesday, "Everything will be okay, baby" as the vet drew blood and ran some tests that showed her white blood cells and t-cell counts had bottomed out. I was told that she needed to stay at the vet's office, where they immediately started her on a couple of antibiotics. They would re-run the blood test in the morning and let me know her prognosis. I told Tuesday, "I'll come get you tomorrow. You'll be fine, don't worry." As she stood there twitching, she sure didn't have a look of "I'll be fine." The next morning, though, she *was* fine. We never did figure out what the problem was, but Tuesday was back playing ball without a twitch.

On the drive home from the vet on that traumatic evening, I had feared the worst. It was strange how Tuesday's twitching brought back memories of another "twitching" event. Boyd Uselton and I had been at the

Waffle House in Plainfield, Indiana, where, over a pot of coffee, we were once again plotting our future. Out of the blue, I got up and boldly walked to the other side of the restaurant, where I introduced myself to a table full of exquisite girls. The next thing I knew I had committed our band to play the following Sunday at their Pentecostal church in Indianapolis. This happened right after the folks at the table next to the girls introduced themselves as the church elders. It is amazing what one will do for a promising date!

When I returned to our table, Boyd asked, "Well, how did you make out?" I told him what I had done, and he pointed out that we didn't even have a band—Boyd and I were a duo at that time called "Roadside Table." We really weren't even a duo—Boyd would play a set and then I would play a set. To bail us out, I now had to convince a couple of Avon, Indiana dudes that Boyd and I had been bandmates within the fabled band called "The Hand Me Downs." This was a band that had conquered Indiana's rural world of rock and roll. Those "trendsetting" places included Lake Bean Blossom, Cuba and Gnaw Bone, Indiana. Yes, we had been the reigning kings—at least in our own minds.

To save myself, I wooed Carl "The Moose" Allen on guitar and Mardy "The Chick Slayer" Wilson on drums. Their response was "You did what, Rogers? You are more brain dead than we thought!" When I pointed out that we would only have to play three songs, they reluctantly came on board. "Rogers, you owe us big time now." I am still working that one off. We worked up The Byrds song, "Jesus Is Just Alright" (later recorded by the Doobie Brothers), a song Boyd and I wrote called, "Lord, I'm So Weary" (about a guy on death row), and reworked the Spencer Davis Group song from "Gimme Some Loving" to "Gimme Some Jesus."

Come show time we were all a little nervous. None of us had ever been in a Pentecostal church before, let alone played Pentecostal rock and roll. One of the church elders informed me that there would be a hymn followed by a prayer. He would then introduce us. I was to go to the pulpit and give my sermon. He told me he was thrilled that a young man such as I was walking in the light. I had failed to mention the sermon part of our show to my bandmates. When I told them, they all screeched in unison, "You're doing what?".

After our introduction I found myself standing at the pulpit with a completely blank mind--although that was no different from normal for me. I suddenly blurted out, "And now Boyd Uselton will deliver the sermon that you have all been waiting to hear tonight." I walked back to my guitar. Boyd, whose frantic eyes looked like those of a wild beast caught in high-beam headlights with no place to run, slowly walked up to the pulpit to a congregational chorus of "Praise the Lord!" He spoke about five words and passed out cold, falling down from the pupit. He lay there under the cross, twitching away. The congregation erupted with cheers of "Hallelujah!" and "Sweet Jesus!" People began running up to Boyd, laying hands on him, looking to the heavens with a vociferous "Praise Jesus!" There were people running around the sanctuary speaking in tongues, a new language for me.

Carl was found hiding behind his guitar amp, tightly squeezing his beloved Rickenbacker twelve-string guitar as if the end were near. Today he is a very religious man. Mardy sat paralyzed behind his drum-set fortress. As for me, I wondered, as Boyd slowly stirred and came around, might he be ticked off? But he passed out again, and went on twitching.

There are a great many other things that can cause one to develop an uncontrollable or involuntary twitch, such as a tax audit, flashing red lights in your rearview mirror, a court subpoena, or finding out that your job has just moved offshore. Then there's the eviction notice from the county that might be posted on your front door, to make room for yet another tasteless, cheesy, foreign-owned strip mall. Of course we all know that in Oregon the county really owns your home anyhow. Just try not paying your property taxes and see what happens. You might have developed your twitch after receiving a scorpion sting, a hornet bite, or a kiss from a "no-see-um" gnat. Or after the Wall Street bankers rewrote the bankruptcy laws for everyone but themselves, followed by new legislation that will bail them out of the subprime lending fiasco that they created. Oh yes, that bailout will be with our tax dollars. Maybe your twitch started about the time you realized how under-reported the inflation rate really is in America. Maybe your twitch started when you figured out that our security has been sold to China. This sellout has allowed the moneychangers to build themselves a bigger Wall Street money vault.

Just recently it was me who developed a sudden twitch—after reading the quote below. I realized how close to reality these word currently echo. This has happened because we have let it!

"I believe that banking institutions are more dangerous to our liberties than standing armies. If the American people ever allow private banks to control the issue of their currency...the banks and corporations that will grow up around them will deprive the people of their property until their children wake up homeless on the continent their fathers conquered. The issuing power should be taken from the banks and restored to the people, to whom it properly belongs."

—Thomas Jefferson, Letter to the Secretary of the Treasury Albert Galatin (1802)

Poppies, Iris, and Applegate Folks

Tuesday is insisting that I throw her tennis ball every thirty seconds or so. She loves to leap into the air and snag her favorite toy. Utah likes to play ball, too, but he's no match for Tuesday. She'll make four or five catches to every one of his. If Boogie were still here, well, she wouldn't have been bothered with such trivial things as catching the ball. She would have been busy trying to figure out a new way to open our refrigerator door and help herself to a feast made for a queen.

Looking out on the garden from the swing, I am amazed at how beautiful the spring flowers are this year. Our red poppies are over four feet tall. We have hundreds and hundreds of columbines in bloom, covering a rainbow of colors. Our Russell lupines and bearded iris look like a smorgasbord of tasty desserts. The roses are just peeking through their buds and the delphiniums are reaching for the sky.

Yes sir, it is a blessing for my wife Sioux and me to have such a beautiful garden. It's like living in our own park. We have many plants that have naturalized, such as the orange poppies that grow next to the lavender iris. This color combination isn't one I would have necessarily planned, but my, oh my, how well the two colors complement each other.

This gets me to thinking about the people of the Applegate, folks who are as different in their ways of life as the flowers in our garden—some dominant, some passive, some bold, and some shy. When you mix all these different people together, and if they take the time to find ideas they can agree on, rather than concentrating on what they disagree about, you'll be amazed at what a community can accomplish. Nothing is insurmountable. Like our orange poppies and lavender iris, you never know which folks will roll up their sleeves, stand shoulder to shoulder, and say, "This needs doing." And they'll look good doing it.

Tuesday and Utah take a break from herding chickens to pose for photo, 2003.